Breathtaking

A NOVEL

C. S. Challinor

Reprint (previously *Pink Champagne on Ice*)

Cover art © Can Stock Photo, Inc., 2012

Book cover, design, and production by Perfect Pages Literary Management, Inc.

This is a work of fiction. All of the names, characters, places, and events in this novel are either the product of the author's imagination or are used fictitiously, and any resemblance to actual persons, whether living or deceased, is entirely coincidental.

ISBN-13: 978-1477526606
ISBN-10: 1477526609

OTHER TITLES BY AUTHOR

Remember, remember

The Fifth of November;

The Gunpowder, Treason and Plot!

—Anonymous English cautionary rhyme

Prologue

*K*athy reached into a file cabinet behind her desk and pulled a Fla-Bar sales contract from a hanging folder. "Here, hon, take this one. I'll print up some more."

"Thanks." Angelica snatched a pen from the desk. "What's the date today?"

"November fifth."

Angelica dated the contract and slid the form in her briefcase.

"By the way, a gift came for you," Kathy said. "It's on your desk."

Angelica perked up at the news. "Really? Who's it from?"

"Haven't a clue. Looks pretty, though. I found it on my desk with a note saying, *'For Angelica.'*"

Puzzled, Angelica made for her cubicle. Could it be she had a secret admirer? Or perhaps it was a token of appreciation from a satisfied customer. She had received cookies and bath accessories in the past, even a crate of pears. With a quiver of anticipation, she entered her workspace and beheld a box on her desk wrapped in silver paper and topped with a festive orange bow. She picked up the gift, which was quite light. Definitely not bubble bath or foot massage lotion, she concluded.

Jenn, passing by with a mug of steaming coffee, asked if she was going to open it.

Angelica hesitated. "I thought I'd wait until I got home."

"You think it might be some naughty lingerie?" Jenn lowered her voice as she leaned against the partition wall, cradling her mug. "Ooh, how exciting! Please open it," she begged. "I swear I won't tell."

Angelica shot her a conspiratorial grin. "Oh, alright then. The suspense is killing me too."

The only other people she could imagine sending her a gift were her family, but this box had not come in the mail. She searched for a card and, finding none, peeled off the bow and removed the decorative paper. Beneath, she found a plain green cardboard box. She popped open the lid, and *BOOM!*

As the gift exploded, someone in the office screamed, and Jenn's mug hit the floor. Silver stars attached to red and yellow streamers erupted into the air. Smoke billowed toward the ceiling.

Broker Bob flew out of his office, mopping his pale domed brow with a red silk handkerchief. "Wha-what happened?" he shrilled, competing in pitch with the smoke detector alarm. "Is anything damaged? Is anyone hurt? Remember, you can't sue!"

Angelica stood rooted to the floor of her cubicle. Kathy rushed to her side. Once the alarm piped down into protracted squeaks, everybody started talking at once.

"That was no ordinary smoke bomb," croaked Bill Bungle, a veteran of Korea, feebly waving away wisps of smoke.

Broker Bob glared at the multicolor streamers strewn on the carpet. "Will someone please tell me what the dickens is going on here?"

"I opened the box and it exploded," Angelica explained, picking up debris from the floor. " '*Remember, remember the fifth of November,*' " she read aloud from the inside of the lid.

"Well, no one's very likely to forget it now," Broker Bob

retorted.

" *'Gunpowder, treason and plot!* " she finished quoting from the old English verse.

"What? Who did the box come from?"

Angelica recalled where she had heard the rhyme before. "From Peter Bedford, my Plovers Key client. I think he was just throwing a prank on his birthday."

"I see," Broker Bob said in a tight voice. "Your client has a weird sense of humor."

"He's British."

"Aren't you meeting with a prospect at his condo this morning?"

"Yes, and I best get going." She snatched up her briefcase, glad of the cue to escape. "I'll finish cleaning this up later," she added, gesturing toward the ripped paper and cardboard on the carpet. Not to mention the coffee splatters.

"Just be sure and come back with a signed contract," Broker Bob sputtered before marching back to his office.

Ignoring the curious expressions on her colleagues' faces, and Gloria's gloating one, Angelica flew from the premises. Peter Bedford! What an idiot, she fumed. What was he thinking? She preferred to arrive calm and collected at meetings, not rushed and irate.

Flooring the gas all the way to Plovers Key, she blared her horn at the early snowbirds in their slow-boat Lincolns and Cadillacs, and screeched into the parking space beside Bedford's bronze Aston Martin. The sunroof was open, the sky overcast. Angelica hoped it would rain all over his molded two-tone leather interior.

She strode into the lobby and slammed her fist on the elevator button.

Calm down. This is not the right mindset for closing a sale, she reminded herself, and began practicing deep, slow breathing on the way up to the eighth floor. She smoothed her hair behind her ear and straightened the lapels of her gray jacket. Then, with measured steps, she approached #801 and knocked on the door.

There had better be a good explanation for this, she thought, though for the life of her, she could not imagine what that might be.

1

A month earlier, murder had been the last thing on Angelica's mind as she parked in front of the twelve-story condominium tower, the shell pink stucco girded with white balconies soaring into a cloudless blue October sky.

Digital camera and door key in hand, she stepped into an airy tiled foyer, the surrounding walls affixed with pastel scenes of palms trees, dolphins, and egrets. Bypassing the concierge desk, she made for the elevators, recalling with satisfaction how eager the condo owner had been to sign the listing agreement for a six percent commission. She must have made a good impression on Mrs. Bedford: gray suit, not too short; black pumps, not too high. The perfect ensemble, Angelica complimented herself in retrospect. And the waterfront property was sure to move quickly at such a steal.

The elevator pinged to a stop. At the end of a plush-carpeted corridor, she unlocked the door to #801, viewing it for the second time since her appointment with Mrs. Bedford just two days before. Opening onto a living room decorated in understated chic in subtle shades of brown and beige, the unit showed like a feature out of a home design magazine. Drawn to the view, she drifted to the glass sliders leading out to the balcony. There, between a pair of billowy drapes, the Gulf of Mexico shimmered in variegated shades of blue and green while, in the foreground, white umbrellas dotted the sand.

She cocked an ear. Strange . . . It couldn't be the pounding of surf she was hearing. Not on this coast. Turning away from the balcony, she listened more closely. There it was again, a series of thuds and groans, as though someone were trying to force open a jammed door. And it came from inside the condo, just down the hall. A handyman perhaps?

Best take a look, she thought, moving in that direction. At the door to the master suite, she froze. She could not believe what she saw on the king-size bed. In dismay, she spun around and bolted back down the hall. Mrs. Bedford had flown back to New York with her husband that morning, and no one was supposed to be here, and yet those two seemed very much at home.

She considered dialing her client's Manhattan number, but promptly dismissed the idea. She didn't want to worry Mrs. Bedford the day she left town. She wanted her first call to be about an interested prospect so that her client would recommend the competent young Angelica Lane to wealthy friends looking to snap up property on Southwest Florida's sandy shores before prices soared again.

She stopped by the front desk. "Excuse me," she said, striving for composure. "There seems to be a problem in eight-oh-one."

"What kind of problem?" the male concierge asked, a flick-haired youth with a dimpled chin, whose name badge read, "*Blayne.*"

"There's a couple in there and they're, well, they're . . ."

"What?"

"You know!"

"Dead?"

"No! Very much alive, actually."

"Ain't nobody supposed to be in there. Mrs. Bedford left this morning. And you are?"

"Her Realtor." She proffered her business card.

"I'll check it out, Ms. Lane. Don't you worry about it, 'kay?"

Angelica glared at him. "This is a serious matter."

"Must be someone who had a key," the young man said with a knowing smirk. "Perhaps a friend of Mr. Bedford's."

"Mrs. Bedford never mentioned . . . Oh, never mind! Please, just go up and knock at the door."

"Soon as I get a minute. There must be an innocent explanation."

"Didn't look very innocent to me," she muttered, turning to leave.

Striding to her Camry, she speed-dialed the office manager at Plum Realty.

"You have 'fo-wa' messages," Kathy informed her in her pronounced Bostonian accent. "And your dad wants you to call him. Now, don't worry," she pre-empted. "He sounded fine. And adorable. When do I get to meet him?"

"Soon, I hope," Angelica fudged. He and Kathy were the same age and both divorced. However, her father lived in Hawaii, taking the concept of a long-distance relationship rather too far. "Listen, I'll buy you lunch at Delilah's. I need your advice. Something came up while I was at the Plovers Key condo."

She glanced up at the pink condominium tower rising in phallic grandeur from the parking lot. Her new listing on the eighth floor enjoyed a private southwest-facing balcony with views of both bay and sea. The million-dollar sale would push Rick Powers from the top spot at Plum Realty, she gloated, and she would almost certainly win Bill Bungle's office if she got a contract in time.

In the meantime, what was she supposed to do about the couple in 801? Never in her six years in real estate had she encountered this problem. Perhaps she should have gone back to the unit and knocked, instead of leaving the inept desk clerk to deal with it. But at the time, she had considered discretion the better part of valor. Now she wasn't so sure.

Hopefully, Kathy would know what to do. The office manager usually did.

*****

Taking note of the ash brown hair that flowed to her collar, the man watched Angelica Lane cross the plaza and sit at one of the wrought-iron café tables. An appealing hint of gawkiness lent a vulnerability to her polished demeanor, yet the long body and shiny bob were by far the most noticeable things about her in the flesh. Her picture didn't do her justice. She came across as quite attractive in an earnest sort of way, much like a spokeswoman on a TV commercial. She was definitely a possibility.

The subject consulted her cell phone. A woman in her early fifties with a gray crew-cut and funky pink eyewear joined her at table. They laughed comfortably together and studied their menus.

He waited.

Waiting constituted a major part of this job. It wasn't a job he particularly relished, but he had little choice.

2

Angelica expelled a dramatic sigh as she finished describing the condo incident to Kathy, notably the buxom blonde, her male partner, and the gold watch gleaming between two champagne flutes on the bedside table. She had not been able to make out the man's face.

An empty plate sat before her with the prodded remains of her curry chicken croissant. "So now I have to decide whether to call Mrs. Bedford, which might make me seem incompetent, or else deal with the situation myself."

She checked her phone to see if the concierge had called, even though she had it on vibrate. Blayne-with-a-"y" must surely have had time to go up to the Bedford unit by now.

"In your place, I'd have asked the couple why they were trespassing in my listing," the office manager remarked.

"I didn't know who I was dealing with! And you have no idea how embarrassed I felt."

"They might've been more embarrassed," Kathy pointed out, eyes twinkling behind her translucent pink frames. "Who else has a key to the condo?"

"Mrs. Bedford's husband, I guess. But he's out of town as well. She told me that the management was under strict instructions not to hand the key out to anyone except for cleaning and maintenance purposes. She wants the condo available for showing at a moment's notice."

"Sounds like the lady's in a hurry to sell. I wonder why?" Kathy loved mysteries, especially the cat, quilt and culinary variety, which she devoured in her lunch breaks.

"Apparently it's her husband's idea," Angelica explained. "He came into property in England and wants to spend more time there. Bella Bedford waxed lyrical about a cottage in Coventry, with a garden chock-full of foxglove and hollyhocks." An image that reminded Angelica of a picture-perfect jigsaw puzzle she had assembled as a child.

"So, what is this Bella Bedford like?" Kathy asked, lipstick poised as she squinted into the mirror of her compact.

Angelica cast her mind back to the listing appointment, the one and only time she had met her client. "About your age, I'd guess. Lacquered, mid-length silvery blond hair. Silk shirt, tailored black pants, strings of pearls, and huge diamond studs in her ears."

"Sounds like Krystle Carrington." Kathy patted down her stiff gray brush, and snapping shut her compact, returned it to her purse. "Well, the intruders have probably come up for air by now. And you need to make sure nothing was stolen."

Startled, Angelica looked up from the check she was signing. "You really think they were up to something like that?"

Kathy shrugged her narrow shoulders. "You never know. Perhaps they brought their friends over for an orgy."

"I'll go back first thing tomorrow," Angelica murmured uneasily. "This morning I got stuck behind an Oldsmobile doing twenty in a no-passing zone. It had a plate with '*AM2 100*' on it. I can't face going through that again in one day." Yet even as she spoke she realized she was making excuses. The fact remained she didn't want to run into the rodeo duo again.

"What if they trashed the place?" Kathy suggested.

That did it. Angelica whipped the cell phone from her pocket. "I need you to go check on eight-oh-one right away," she instructed the desk clerk. "What if the place has been trashed or something's gone missing?" she asked, echoing Kathy's suspicions. She heard a put-upon sigh at the other end of the connection. "Call me back at once," she directed, and ended the call.

"What are you going to tell Broker Bob when he asks why the condo isn't listed on MLS yet?" Kathy asked.

"I'll tell him the key wasn't available." Before she input data on the site that agents used to sell and source properties, she needed to take photos and measurements. "Although you know what I'd really like to tell him."

"Yes, well, I wouldn't do that," Kathy said. "Remember how he's always telling everybody how expendable they are?"

"Not Rick."

"Rick is the chief rainmaker."

"That's another reason I want to sell the Plovers Key condo. He's getting way too big for his boots."

They both laughed. Five-seven in his stocking feet, Rick wore lifts in his shoes.

Kathy checked her watch. "Ooops. Best get back to the office."

They left the café and headed to Plum Realty in separate cars. A black SUV snuck up on them, pulling out of the plaza lot and maintaining a cautious distance in the lunch hour traffic on U.S. 41.

3

*P*lum Realty occupied a prime location in north Portofino on the main highway. The green-on-beige storefront unit, visible to southbound traffic, displayed color photos of listings for sale in the windows. Inside the entrance, ten framed portraits of agents covered one wall. Rick, flashing perfect pearly whites, could have been a commercial for cosmetic dentistry. Angelica hated her own shot, which she thought made her look prudish, her pursed smile showing no teeth, her hair limp and dullish brown. She vowed to get it retaken when she had more time.

With the sagging feeling she had not accomplished much that day, she entered her corner cubicle. A pile of research for a couple relocating from Cleveland was next on her list. She picked up her buyers' folder from between the neat stacks of stationery on her desk and proceeded to stare out the window at her uninspiring view of the parking lot, while mulling over the situation at Plovers Key.

The concierge had called as she drove back from lunch to say the condo had been left in immaculate condition. "As if no one was here," is how Blayne put it, implying by his tone that the amorous couple had been a figment of Angelica's imagination. That was a relief, certainly, but it didn't answer the question of who the couple had been, and whether they should have been there in the first place.

Kathy had advised her to call Bella Bedford and explain the situation, but still she hesitated. If no harm had been done, why worry the owner? And the front desk had been alerted. All the same, a niggling doubt remained. Perhaps she had not done all that she should.

"Angelica, you missed our lunch date." Rick Powers' smooth tenor rang out from the opening in the partition.

Sliding into the other chair without so much as a by-your-leave, he deposited his dainty size nines on her desk, a toothpick nodding between even white teeth. Rick could have been a male model, Angelica reflected; had he not been so short.

"We didn't have a lunch date," she reminded him.

"Your loss. Any hits on the Plovers Key condo yet? But I guess it's out of your usual price range, huh?" He folded his arms behind glossy dark hair with precision cut sideburns. "I wonder why your client specified a female agent?"

"I wonder," Angelica said.

"Doing anything fun this evening?"

"I'm taking Hercules for a walk on the beach—if I get through all this paperwork and make it home early enough."

"Hercules?" Rick asked, never one to take a hint.

"My dog."

"Ah, yes. What sort of dog is it again?"

"A Maltese," she replied a touch defensively. So maybe Hercules *was* an oversized name for a ten-pound canine, but he did try to live up to it. Her father, with characteristic dry humor, had named him after the mythical Greek hero. The puppy had been his housewarming gift when she moved into her condo.

"That's one of those small, yappy things, right?"

You're vertically challenged and pretty annoying yourself, Angelica thought. "Look, Rick, I'd love to sit and chat, but I have work to do."

He wagged a finger at her. "All work and no play . . ." He paused, clearly unable to remember the rest. "You want old Bill's office, but I'm still one sale ahead of you, don't forget." Strutting behind her chair in his elevator shoes, he began massaging her shoulders before she could raise an objection. Rick's wandering hands had earned him the nickname Office Octopus among the female agents. "You've got serious knots in your neck, Angelica. You really need to lighten up."

Whistling a tune, he walked out of her cubicle, leaving her more rigid than a cat with its back up, spitting fur. Why he pursued her when she kept rebutting his advances, defied her comprehension. At thirty-seven years of age, single and successful, he had his fair share of girlfriends.

Rick walked a fine line between friendliness and flirtation, and Angelica swore the moment he crossed it she would knee him where it hurt most. She reveled in whimsical anticipation of that moment before landing with a bump on the floor of reality. It was true Rick gadded about and still managed to be top listing and sales agent most months. He generated a lot of business on the golf course, whereas she hated golf with a passion. In fact, she couldn't imagine anything more boring.

But if she sold the luxury condo before Thanksgiving, she would stand a good chance of winning Bill's office, which had the advantage of an actual door. Rick would no longer be able to swagger in and out at will and give her unsolicited back rubs. Besides, he deserved to be brought down a peg or two. She resolved then and there to take the photos of her new listing at Plovers Key the next morning, no matter what she found. And discretion be damned.

4

*S*omeone with a spare key could have snuck up to #801 undetected, Angelica reflected as she drove to Plovers Key the following day, impatient to see if her listing was as the desk clerk had assured her. It wasn't as though he paid much attention. As she walked into the foyer, she observed him slouched behind reception, mindlessly thumbing away at the keypad on his cell phone, probably multi-texting his equally mindless friends.

She rode up the elevator to the eighth floor and this time rang the doorbell and waited before inserting the key in the lock. Once inside, she stood quite still. The condo held its breath, the only sounds the hum of the air conditioning and the murmur of traffic from the beach road. Glancing down the hall, she noted that the king-size bed was made up impeccably. Everything appeared in its place.

So far, so good.

After snapping a few pictures of the master bedroom, she entered the bathroom. The air was humid, a towel folded over the rim of the marble tub felt damp to her touch. Upon pulling back the curtain, she spotted a man's gold watch in a corner, the same timepiece she had seen on the bedside table the previous day. Turning it over in her palm, she read the initials *P.G.B.* inscribed in the eighteen-karat gold. *B* for Bedford? she wondered.

Her client's husband? She hoped not.

The owner would no doubt return to claim such an expensive watch. However, the cleaning staff came in once a week and it might go missing. Angelica decided to leave her business card in the bathroom and on the back wrote, *"Watch found. Please call this number."*

That way she would find out for certain the identity of the man in the bedroom. One thing was for sure: The man's partner had not been Mrs. Bedford. The curvaceous body and cascading blond hair clearly belonged to a younger woman.

In the meantime, other business demanded Angelica's attention. The Peyntons in Cleveland were due to arrive soon and expected a shortlist of properties to view. She would have to visit a least a dozen beforehand.

She returned to the office to pursue her search on the multiple listing site, arriving in time to hear Broker Bob ring the gong, signifying a new sale. Her heart missed a beat. Another sale for Rick? She rushed to Kathy's desk.

"Patti's," the office manager said before she could ask.

That was alright. Patti did not constitute a threat for Bill's office. She was a part-timer, in spite of Broker Bob's best efforts to convert her, and mainly brokered deals for friends and family.

By the end of the day, Angelica had forgotten all about the gold watch, the Peyntons, and office politics. She looked forward to getting home and changing out of her suit into a comfortable cotton tee and a pair of sweat pants. Driving up to the Cascades, she pressed the black box attached to her sun visor, and the gate opened to a small community of carriage homes set among manicured lawns, mini waterfalls, and subtropical shrubs, reminding her of Hawaii. The sight of her condo, purchased pre-construction, never ceased to fill her with pleasure and pride.

Passing the mailboxes located by the communal pool, she stopped the car and rolled down her window. A violet envelope with a Los Angeles postmark awaited her in her slot.

"Jelly," began the note. Only her sister called her by that ridiculous name. *"I really need to talk to you. I can't keep this to myself any longer. Miss you—Claire."*

The adventurous and extrovert one, Claire had headed West to pursue a career in cosmetology. What could have prompted the letter? And why couldn't she phone or text like everyone else? But then, Claire had always had a flair for the dramatic, much like their mother. If her sister needed urgent help, she would have called, Angelica decided. It really was too much sending a provocative message by snail mail.

As soon as she reached the concrete steps to her second-story condo, she heard Hercules yapping away in excitement through the front door, desperate to be let out on his walk. The phone call to her sister would have to wait. Parting the dog's white fur, soft and feathery as plumage, she attached the leash hanging from a rack in the hallway and straightened the blue bow on his topknot. Once on the path, he trotted in front of her, periodically darting into the lush foliage. When they reached the biggest tree on the lawn, he lifted his leg and fertilized the roots thoroughly. Angelica's cell phone trilled in her pocket.

"Peter Bedford here," the caller announced.

Bedford, Bedford, thought Angelica, thrown for a moment by the British accent and distracted by Claire's note.

"Y-yes!" she said, suddenly placing him. "How can I help you?"

"It appears you have my watch."

Then it was indeed Mrs. Bedford's husband she had seen in the master bedroom at Plovers Key. Heat rushed to her face as she fought down her confusion. "Yes, of course," she managed to reply. "So, you're in town?"

"I postponed my flight. I had some outstanding business to attend to."

I'll just bet, Angelica said to herself, wondering if his wife knew all about his outstanding business. "I thought it safest to remove the watch from the condo, since people will be viewing it shortly," she explained in her most professional tone. "Would you like to pick it up from the office tomorrow?"

"That sounds like an awfully dreary plan, doesn't it?" Mr. Bedford replied after a pause. "What about getting together somewhere more congenial?"

Angelica pressed the phone hard to her ear, not sure if she was hearing correctly, and trying not to sound breathless as Hercules dragged her along the path in pursuit of a squirrel. "What do you mean?" she asked. Was he propositioning her? He had never seen her, as far as she knew.

"Are you out jogging?" he asked.

"As a matter of fact, I am." A jog sounded motivated and energetic.

"It sounds like you're running in heels." The thought appeared to entertain Mr. Bedford immensely.

"Really?" Angelica stepped onto the grass where her heel snagged on a root, sending her sprawling into a trimmed hibiscus bush. Swearing under her breath, she reeled Hercules back in on his retractable lead, wishing she had changed shoes before walking the dog.

"Did you fall?" Bedford inquired.

"No, I just stopped to rest. Look, Mr. Bedford, about your watch—"

"I'll be at Plovers Key in the morning," he said. "Bring it to me there, would you? I'm sure you have measurements to take, and whatnot. Eleven o'clock?"

How could she refuse her most important client? And she had to get off the phone before Hercules started yapping. "Eleven o'clock," she agreed.

"Good. And, Ms. Lane? Next time you go running, wear appropriate shoes?"

Angelica thought she heard a chuckle before the connection was broken.

Hercules frolicked about her, running up only to bound away before she could catch him. Yet for all her effort at playfulness, she felt oddly disquieted. Mr. Bedford seemed nice enough, if a bit patronizing, but something felt wrong.

Perhaps tomorrow would provide an innocent explanation for what she had witnessed at the condo, or at least some sort of clarification. It could be the Bedfords had "an arrangement." Or they were getting divorced—the real reason for selling. She only hoped Bella wasn't completely in the dark about the other woman. Angelica didn't relish being an accomplice to Peter Bedford's sordid little secret.

She grabbed Hercules and hurried back to her condo to call Claire, curious to find out what her unpredictable sister had been dying to tell her.

5

"**B**ut Peter!" the woman wailed on the other end of the connection as Peter Bedford pictured her at a swank salon getting a pampered pedicure. "You promised!"

He sighed in frustration. Why did it always turn out this way? Women, however alluring to begin with, inevitably morphed into high-maintenance harpies. He should have known better with Lindy, of all females.

"Sweet-Nuts," she lisped. "How about later then, at the condo?"

Raking a weary hand through his hair, he flopped onto the white kid leather sofa. "Tell you what, Lindy. I'll meet you there at nine before my meeting with the Realtor. How does that sound?"

A resigned sigh. "I guess . . ."

He snapped his cell phone shut and fixed himself a scotch. Where had all the fun gone? Life used to irradiate vibrant color, every day a new adventure offering a challenge or conquest of some sort. Now he felt bored. Tossing two chenille cushions off the sofa, he stretched out and yawned. He was going to be fifty-three soon and should be content with what he'd achieved. He had made all the money he needed, put three kids through college, and married Miss Arkansas 1977. Not a trophy wife exactly, but still glamorous.

Trophy wife. Why did the Yanks have to turn everything

into a sports analogy? He couldn't count the meetings where someone had stepped up to the plate, run with the ball, or else dropped the bloody thing and let the team down. Sometimes he had to wonder if they were discussing business executives or else giving a baseball commentary.

He chucked two more suffocating cushions onto the floor. Maynard's showcase home, decorated by Lindy at a cost that left even Bella astounded, closed in around him, its excess of soft furnishings sucking the air out of his lungs. Even the prospect of his morning rendezvous with Lindy failed to excite him, but he feared what the little vixen might do if he broke off with her. Besides which, she was useful. One thing he had learned about women was that good sex made for a lot of pillow talk, five per cent of which, in Lindy's case, proved worth listening to—and he couldn't afford not to listen with so much at stake.

At least with his wife back in Manhattan he had one less stress to deal with. He would see if he could interest the house agent in lunch, assuming she lived up to the photo printed on her card. Yes, he looked forward to meeting her. She had sounded so polite and vulnerable on the phone. Very proper.

The next day, following his assignation with Lindy, and while waiting for Ms. Lane, he sat on his condo balcony, gazing away through the railings at the mangrove bay to the south, although he was not, in reality, appreciating the view. He was brooding about the birthday card he had received from his wife that morning, an oversized card with a display of fireworks on the front and the words, *'It's your Birthday!'* jeering at him in jolly silver letters.

Fifty-three years *old*. Hell, he hated to be reminded of it. No doubt Bella had sent the card early on purpose. She'd always had a penchant for getting back at him in subtly devious ways. Flipping the card face down on the glass-top table, he poured himself a glass of white wine. A minute later, he checked his sports watch: "10:53." *Balls!* Why was everything fifty-three all of a sudden?

In the parking lot below, a white sedan swung into the reserved visitor space on the far side of his Aston Martin, and a young woman stepped out on the driver's side. Even from his bird's eye view, he could see she was slender. Her copper hair rippled back from her face in the sultry breeze. An effect of the sunlight, he surmised, consulting the photo on her business card where her hair was darker. Black pleated skirt swaying above her knees, she crossed the parking lot, while he followed with his eyes, experiencing the old familiar thrill of the chase.

6

Angelica pressed the elevator button. The prospect of meeting Peter Bedford tied her stomach in a knot. She sincerely hoped that, in light of what she knew about him, he wouldn't embark on his marital problems.

It always amazed her how many of her clients confided about their private lives, probably because their homes usually formed not only their largest financial asset, but also their most emotionally vested one. In some cases, the reason for selling a home was loss of a job; in others, the last kid moving out, and the futile expense of rattling around in a house that felt empty. Oftentimes, the reason was divorce. In this case, she would steer Bedford off any personal topic out of deference to his wife who, after all, had been the one to retain her services.

No reason why the mystery blonde couldn't remain a mystery. No reason for the situation to explode before she sold the condo. She had come to the conclusion it was really none of her business.

With a deep intake of breath, she rang the bell.

"Enter," boomed an English voice from beyond the front door.

Stepping into the living room, Angelica looked around. Something was different somewhere, but she couldn't quite put her finger on it. On the balcony, an athletic, ruddy-complexioned man, whom she immediately recognized in his clothes, paced about, talking on his cell phone. Flicking open the catches on her briefcase, she removed the gold watch.

"Come on through, Miss Lane," he called out, hair glowing a burnished gold in the sun.

"Mr. Bedford, how are you?" She held out her hand.

"Quite well," he said. "Care for some wine? It's so pleasant out I thought we could enjoy the view."

Angelica sat down when he did. "It's a bit early for me," she demurred. "But thanks anyway."

"I insist. It's quite good. Crisp, yet with a round, fruity flavour. And nicely chilled."

"Just half a glass then, thank you."

He filled it to the top. "To selling the condo," he said, raising his glass. "Ah, you have my watch. I must have left it in the shower when I was redoing the grout." He smiled, his hazel eyes and boyish features betraying no sign of a lie. "A gift from my father the year I graduated from Cambridge. Seems like a lifetime ago."

He prattled on about punts and cricket and, by and by, Angelica felt the tension ebb from her body, helped along by the wine. Perhaps Rick was right: She should try to relax more. After all, making nice with clients was all part of the job.

"I have a birthday coming up on November fifth. 'Remember, remember the fifth of November; gunpowder, treason and plot!' Does that poem mean anything to you, Ms. Lane?"

Angelica shook her head in trepidation. She hated quizzes. The answers were always at the tip of her tongue, but never seemed to want to make it all the way out of her mouth.

"Americans are curiously ignorant about British history," Bedford opined. "Except when it comes to chucking our tea into Boston Harbor and ridding this great land of our glorious red coats."

She stifled a yawn. The wine made her sleepy. "You said something about treason and November fifth," she said, expressing polite interest.

"Ah, yes. It's an old English nursery rhyme warning children about Guy Fawkes."

Angelica had a vague recollection of the name in connection with fireworks, due to the fact that a picture she had created in elementary school, in an explosion of red and orange crayon, had won first prize. The rest of the details eluded her. The blank in her mind must have reflected on her face, for Bedford went on to explain.

"Guy Fawkes tried to blow up the Houses of Parliament in sixteen hundred and five during a plot to overthrow King James I and restore the Catholic monarchy. The guards at Westminster Palace, tipped off by an anonymous letter, caught him red-handed with a stockpile of explosives. He was later hanged, drawn and quartered, his head stuck on a pike at the Tower of London for all to see, while the crows pecked out his eyes. Each year, communities in the United Kingdom build a bonfire and burn an effigy of the traitor, or martyr, depending on your point of view."

"What a quaint tradition," Angelica said, thinking it sounded barbaric.

"See this middle initial?" Bedford held out the gold watch she had placed on the table. "The *G* is for Guy."

"Your wife said you wished to spend more time in England?"

"Yes. We have a cottage there. Have you ever visited England?"

"A brief trip to London when I was a kid."

Her family had toured the historical sites on an open top double-decker bus one atypically hot summer day, lapping up the ice cream on their cones before it could drip on their clothes.

"Mrs. Castle maintains the cottage in our absence, but she's getting on now and can't manage it. It's more of a large house than a cottage, really. Originally a dowager's residence. Very old and full of character. Bella adores it. I'll still have business in the States, though."

"And what do you do?" Angelica asked, knowing how much successful male clients enjoyed discussing their work.

"I dabble in the stock market, that sort of thing." Bedford gave a dismissive brush of his hand. "Before that, I was a pilot for Northern Atlantic."

Angelica could easily picture Bedford in a gold-braided captain's hat now that he mentioned it. The scalloped folds behind his ears bespoke the gravitational pull of a thousand take-offs.

"My father is a helicopter pilot," she contributed. "He flies tourists around the island of Kauai."

"Does he, indeed? And does the rest of your family live in Hawaii?"

"My mother remarried last year and moved to Portland. My sister's in L.A."

"My goodness, you're all over the map. Does your sister look like you?"

"Oh, she's ten times prettier," Angelica answered in all candor.

"I find that hard to believe."

Feeling it was time to get back to business, she told Bedford she had a showing the next day.

"Excellent. My wife said you were the most thorough of the agents she interviewed. She's absolutely convinced you're the right girl for the job. Now then, there's something I want to show you in the master bedroom."

Surely not. Angelica had seen quite enough of Mr. Bedford in the master bedroom.

"Come along," he insisted good-humoredly when she

hesitated.

Covering her reluctance, she followed him down the hall and into the bedroom. It was warm in the condo and she felt light-headed from the wine, which she was not used to drinking in the middle of the day. In fact, she rarely drank much at all.

Bedford crossed to the other side of the bed and peered between the horizontal blinds on the window. "Look," he said, pointing.

A bird with a black-speckled breast was perched on the balcony rail preening its rust plumage. "What is it?" she asked standing beside her client.

"A bird of prey of some sort, a young kestrel perhaps. He's been here since I arrived. Probably just taking a breather. Have you ever wondered what it must be like to fly and feel the rush of air against your body?"

Angelica felt herself sway.

"Steady," Bedford said, reaching for her shoulders.

"I'm fine," she assured him. "A touch of vertigo, that's all." They were eight floors up, the bay and mangroves far below them.

His chin leveled her brow. The scent of peppery lemon cologne wafted around him. "I shouldn't have made you have that wine. I'm sorry."

Bedford, she felt sure, was not sorry at all, and did not remove his hands. He slipped them down her silk sleeves and drew her toward him. As Angelica lifted her head to protest, his mouth came down on hers, his tongue parting her lips.

A surprised moan escaped from the back of her throat. His hands were in her hair, hands that had guided commercial jets across continents. She had never French-kissed a man this much more mature. Or a foreign man, for that matter. His fingers trailed down her jaw, thumbs massaging the sweet spot beneath her ears. Another person, not Angelica, responded to his hungry tongue and prying fingers, her head tilted back by the kiss. Oh, but she was kissing Mrs. Bedford's husband. She must stop. Now. This instant!

His hands traced the modest mounds of her blouse. She felt the top button give way. Think professional, she commanded herself. Think listing! Think Rick Powers! That did it. Grasping Bedford's upper arms, she pushed him away, their lips parting with an audible *smack*.

"We can forget this ever happened—if you'd rather," Bedford said, stepping back smartly.

"That might be best," Angelica stammered. Dazed and breathless, she made her excuses, and circumventing the bed, fled the condo for the second time in three days.

She rode the elevator to the lobby in a numb state of shock. One moment she and Peter Bedford had been sipping white wine and making polite conversation. The next, he had been trying to take off her clothes. He made Rick look like a monk. Reaching her car, she glanced up at the tower. Bedford stood on the balcony, his face a blur as he raised his glass to her in a toast.

She sped out of the lot, putting as much distance between herself and Bedford as possible, trying to outrun her shame.

*****

From the shade of a royal palm, the driver of the black SUV watched her rush from the building in a state of disarray. Maybe she was late for an appointment. But wait. The top button of her blouse was undone. So, she had fallen into the trap, after all. Bedford hadn't wasted much time. As usual.

7

"**Y**ou *kissed* him?" Kathy parroted in surprise, a glass of iced tea suspended mid-air. "Mr. Bedford, as in Mrs. Bedford's husband? Your client?"

At the table behind her, a harassed woman argued with a pimply teenage boy reluctant to relinquish his iPad. "Well, it was more a question of him kissing me," Angelica explained.

"But how did it *happen?*"

"I had a glass of wine with him."

"Wine? You mean at the condo? In the *morning?*"

"It was almost lunchtime. Is that so bad?"

"No. But, Angelica, drinking wine with a man you recently met—a *married* man and a *client*, don't forget—and *kissing* him! It just sounds so unlike you."

Angelica slid down her chair and covered her face with her hands. "I know," she groaned. "I have no idea what came over me."

"You barely touched your salad, hon. You okay? You look a tad peaky."

Angelica pushed her plate aside. "What if Bedford blackmails me? He could threaten to pull the listing out from under me if I don't do what he wants. He could lie and tell his wife that I came onto *him!*"

Kathy winced. "Ouch. Does he seem the type to pull a dirty trick like that?"

"I don't know. But we know he was cheating on his wife.

He's obviously a player. He might even have drugged my wine."

"You need to get yourself out of this mess," the office manager declared.

"How?"

"Keep him at arm's length. String him along until the condo is sold."

"He called to ask me to dinner." Angelica braced herself for Kathy's reaction.

"And you refused, of course."

"Not exactly." Angelica studied her pale pink manicure.

"What were you thinking? Are you falling for this guy? Of course not," Kathy answered her own question. "You're too sensible."

"He never mentioned what happened between us. He just said he has a colleague interested in buying a winter home in the area. A big place on the Gulf."

"He'd have to be a multimillionaire to afford that."

"Apparently he owns the largest pet food company in Florida. At least, that's what Peter Bedford said on the phone."

"You think it's a hoax?"

"I wouldn't put it past him. But what if it's legit?" Her commission would be huge.

Kathy glanced at her watch. "We best get the check."

"Rick wines and dines with clients all the time," Angelica pointed out, reaching into her bag. "If I don't go after it, someone else will. There are, after all, thousands of hungry Realtors in this town, as Broker Bob likes to remind us."

"That doesn't mean you have to hop into bed with your client. And that's where this is headed, believe me. Bedford didn't waste much time, did he?"

Angelica opened her purse. "You're right. I'll tell him I'd be grateful if he refers me to his colleague, but that dinner is out of the question. See what happens." She spoke with bravado, but dreaded the prospect of making the call. Peter Bedford was a hard man to say no to, and she suspected she wouldn't want to get on his wrong side.

Throughout the rest of the afternoon, she postponed contacting him, finding one excuse after another to delay the call. It was six by the time she finally summoned up enough courage before she left the office.

"I can't make dinner," she blurted. "But if you could give your colleague my card, I'd really appreciate it," she added lamely.

"Of course," he said. "Sorry you're unavailable. Perhaps another time."

Regretful thoughts gnawed at her that night. What if Bedford had been serious about putting her in contact with his rich colleague? Well, she had burned that bridge when she canceled their date. At least he'd been civil, without actually committing himself to the referral, leaving her dangling like the miniature hula doll on her dad's rearview mirror.

Tossing and turning on the bed, she let her mind dwell on the man who had kissed her as she had never been kissed in all her thirty years. Why was it so hot in the room? She yanked the chain on the ceiling fan and flopped back on the covers. A cooling breeze spiraled above her. Her thoughts spiraled. If she had not stopped Bedford, he would have continued undoing the buttons of her blouse . . .

At that moment, Hercules trundled up his special ramp to the bed and moon-walked over the comforter. Wisps of white hair fell into his doleful brown eyes as he regarded her quizzically, muzzle on his paws.

"I may have made the most expensive mistake of my life," Angelica confided to him.

A beach home in Southwest Florida could be worth tens

of thousands to her in commission. She would be set for the coming year. But Peter Bedford was married and, for all his English charm and debonair virility, he was old enough to be her father. Besides which, it would be unethical from a professional standpoint. She decided to put the matter from her mind. She had taken the high road and would see where it led her.

8

*T*he next day, Angelica had her Cleveland clients sign a buyer's agreement before putting them in her car and showing them property. Over the years, too many house hunters had ended up purchasing with other agents, thus wasting her time and gas, and Angelica had a premonition that Dick and Diane Peynton would be taxing on both. The car's suspension groaned under their weight, confirming her worst fears from the outset.

The couple sported matching T-shirts with big red hearts proclaiming love for their home state of Ohio. Diane's Eau Fatale clashed with Angelica's Kick-Butt Air Freshener, the combined effect threatening to live up to their names and asphyxiate all three of them, until she rolled down the windows. Diane, in the passenger seat, complained that the draft was mussing up her newly frosted bangs. Dick took advantage of the open window to smoke, blowing ash back into the car. Angelica took pride in the as-new condition of her vehicle, and listened with enmity as Dick explained at length that he was in pharmaceuticals, and a promotion had landed him a position in Southwest Florida.

"No more shoveling snow," he said with glee.

The times she had heard that line, Angelica thought.

"It'll be like a permanent vacation," Diane Peynton inserted. "Trix is sure to love it."

"Your dog?" Angelica inquired, relieved to find some

common ground.

"She is kinda," Dick said from the backseat.

"Trix is my mother." Diane swiveled around in a furious jingle of costume jewelry.

"She interferes in everything we do," Dick added, ignoring her stony glare. "The only reason she's not with us now is my company paid for the flight, and she requires two seats to accommodate her humongous rear end. We're gonna need extra wide doors in the house for when she visits."

His wife snorted. "For your beer gut, ya mean, if you stand sideways."

"And, remember, it's gotta have a large garage and be close to a golf course," Dick specified.

"Yes, I took all those criteria into account," Angelica said. "You'll find that Portofino has the best golf courses."

"The shopping better be good," Diane muttered.

"Excellent shopping," Angelica assured her. "And lots of big malls."

"For big people?" Dick laughed. "Wanna hear a mother-in-law joke?"

Angelica politely refused. She could not wait for the day to be over. However, she had lined up five houses for them to view and had promised them lunch, an offer she already regretted.

During the course of the day, the Peyntons found fault with each and every one of the homes. Too poky, too exposed, too old, too expensive. Back in Cleveland, Dick protested at each showing, you got a lot more bang for your buck, even in this lousy economy. What price sunshine? Angelica countered. And beaches? And lifestyle?

She decided to throw in a furnished builder's spec, which was out of the Peyntons' price range, but matched their requirements. Sometimes buyers found the extra funds from somewhere. Dick had hinted that Trix had money, and only her daughter to leave it to. Plus the house had a lockbox on the door and, being vacant, was easy to show.

The rooms were spacious and the ceilings high, the fixtures and fittings of good quality, and everything in its place, including framed photos of models posing as family, and fake laptops and fruit, to give the place a lived-in feel. Diane gushed and Dick griped, until he saw the two-car garage, finished down to the smooth floor.

"Now this is what I call a garage." With a satisfied air, he looked about him through his yellow-tinted glasses. "What did you say the price tag was?"

Angelica repeated the price of the home. The builder was offering a bonus to Realtors as an incentive to move it. "The furniture's included."

"What if we don't want the furniture?"

"Perhaps we can come to some arrangement with the builder, and he can put it in his next model."

"I like the idea of having everything new," Diane said as they returned to the living room. She dropped into a capacious sofa. "It would save us having to haul all our stuff down from Cleveland."

"Even if the builder lopped a hundred gees off the price, we still couldn't afford it."

Diane pouted. "I thought you were getting a raise."

"Not that big of a one." Sweat beaded the sunburned crown of Dick's balding head and glistened in the matted fur surrounding his squat neck.

Finally, as Angelica was driving her disgruntled clients back to the office, she received a call from Peter Bedford.

"We can't leave this hanging in the air," he told her. "We have the business of selling Plovers Key."

"I understand," Angelica murmured into her phone. "This will certainly not interfere with your condom."

"Condom?" Bedford guffawed. "Did you say condom?"

"Did she really say condom?" Dick asked his wife.

"Of course not." Angelica switched the cell phone to her left ear. "I said condominium."

"So we'll have dinner and discuss the matter," Bedford dictated.

"Can I call you back? I'm with clients right now."

"*La Chandelle* on Silver Sands. I'm sure you know the place. Seven this evening suit you?"

"As you wish, Mr. Bedford." Anything to get him off the phone.

"Oh, do stop acting as though you're Little Miss Riding Hood and I'm the big bad wolf. I won't eat you."

"Seven is fine," Angelica said in a hurry. "See you there."

She ended the call and checked the dashboard clock. They were stuck in rush hour traffic, Dick Peynton having insisted on pacing each garage three times and making copious notes.

"The last property had the biggest garage," he said, revisiting the topic. "Gotta have a decent sized garage."

"If a garage means so much to you," his wife told him, "why don't you just find one and live in it?" She turned to Angelica. "We could convert the garage into a suite for my mother, I guess."

"Where would I put all my power tools?"

"Up your—"

"I'm sure we can come up with a solution," Angelica said diplomatically, desperate to be rid of her clients and conscious of valuable time slipping by. She still had to get home and change, and see to her dog. She dropped her clients back off at the office and urged them to reconsider the day's properties, reminding them that the first five homes they had seen were the best value she had managed to find on their particular budget and with their specific requirements in view.

Back at the Cascades, she stripped off her clothes and

filled the cultured marble tub. She had been looking forward to a relaxing soak all day, but needed to be at the restaurant in less than an hour. Bedford had certainly picked an out-of-the-way place, she reflected. Come to think of it, La Chandelle on Silver Sands Beach was not that far from his Plovers Key lair. She considered canceling dinner again. Only, that might blow the existing listing, and she couldn't risk that, especially with the contest for Bill's office hanging in the balance. In the top corner of the mirror, two columns of numbers written in red lipstick showed the month's sales. Rick still led by one. Plovers Key could be her ticket to success, and a juicy referral from Peter Bedford for another big property would be the cherry on the icing.

In any case, she and Bedford were meeting in a public place and she could leave whenever she wanted.

As she got out of the bath, she caught sight of herself in the mirror. "Angelica-Spindelica!" her sister used to tease, comparing her to a clothespin. She felt tempted to try Claire's number before she left, but there was no time for the heart-to-heart talk her sister had hinted at in her brief letter.

Angelica brushed out her hair, and applied eyeliner, mascara, a dab of powder, and lip-gloss. She stepped into a black lace dress with a scooped neck and slipped her feet into a pair of kitten-heel pumps. With a final, nervous glance at her reflection, she switched off the light.

"Sorry, Herx, no time for a walk this evening," she said, plunking the dog in his litter box, to which he replied with an indignant grunt.

Grabbing her purse and keys, she flew out the front door. A fluttery bird swooped in her stomach. Perhaps she should have taken Kathy's advice. Wracked with misgivings, she cruised along the coast road, making good time to the restaurant and hoping Peter Bedford was not leading her down the proverbial garden path.

9

Angelica spotted Bedford's Aston Martin DB9 parked in front of the restaurant, the sleek bronze body gleaming in the last rays of the sun. Two valet attendants stood drooling over it, discussing its maximum speed of 186 miles per hour and matching price tag, times one thousand. The cost of a four-bedroom house, Angelica thought as she passed. The young men glanced at her in fleeting approval, their attention immediately riveted back to the two-door coupe.

She felt awkward entering the restaurant alone. "I'm here to meet Peter Bedford," she told the hostess at the podium in a businesslike voice that sounded acutely at odds with her form-fitting dress. She regretted now not having worn a suit.

A man in tails materialized by her side and led her through a dining room where soft jazz floated among tables decorated with dewy pink roses. In a corner of a veranda overlooking the white sand beach, Bedford sat perusing a menu, his watch gleaming in the candlelight. He half rose, eyes feasting upon her. A ginger tom within paw strike of a canary could not have appeared more smug.

"A cocktail, *madame?*" the maître d' inquired upon seating her.

"Just an iced water for now, thank you," Angelica replied.

"A kir royale for the lady," Bedford instructed the maître d'. "And another scotch. Beautiful evening, isn't it?" he said to Angelica with an eager-to-please charm that threw her off balance, enough anyway to make her forgive him for undermining her order.

The last of the sun cast a ribbon of gold over the Gulf, silhouetting a sailboat against the horizon. A balmy night breeze caressed her bare arms.

"It's gorgeous," she said. "Do you sail, Mr. Bedford?"

"Peter—please. I have a yacht I keep at the marina. And you?"

"I don't have time, unfortunately."

"You don't have to be semi-retired like myself to go out on the water. Shame not to in Florida. So, what *do* you do in your free time, Angelica?"

"I–ahem, sketch."

"Sketch? As in drawing?" Bedford looked amused. "How very Jane Eyre. And do you play the harpsichord as well?"

Oh, heck. Why hadn't she said rock climbing or kick boxing instead?

"Are you any good?"

"It's just a hobby."

"Never mind, I can tell you're a modest sort of girl. Now then," he went on. "Perhaps you can update me on progress with our sale."

"I'm holding an open house on Sunday to attract the after-brunch crowd," she informed him as a waiter delivered her cocktail, a delicious concoction of champagne imbued with blackcurrant liqueur.

"What happened about the showing you mentioned?"

"Mrs. Van Ries was concerned about traffic noise from the drawbridge."

"But you can barely hear it from the eighth floor, even with the window open."

"I know, but she's an insomniac."

Bedford raised an eyebrow. "Perhaps Mr. Van Ries could knock her out with a sledgehammer. Please. Take a look at the menu and see what you'd like."

Angelica opened the leather-bound menu, alarmed to discover it was written entirely in French, complete with the pesky little accents.

"They have menus with English subtitles if you prefer," he told her. "It just so happens that I read French fluently."

Well, of course you do, Angelica thought. And how like Bedford to put her at a disadvantage.

"Let me know if you need any help," he added.

Having studied two years of basic French in high school, Angelica dissected the print. *Salade* something *au vinaigrette.* Okay, that would do as an appetizer. Now, where was the chicken? *Poissons.* No, that was fish. Ah! *Ris de veau.* Rice of something. A risotto perhaps.

Bedford smiled urbanely. "I think everyone should learn at least enough French to be able to order off a menu, don't you agree?"

"Absolutely," Angelica said. "As a mark of respect to the French, who came up with all this wonderful cuisine."

"I must say," her client continued, "I find it ironical that the Americans who are the world's worst linguists find it necessary to pronounce 'herb' like the French, dropping the *h*, and yet they can't seem to bring themselves to actually spell it the French way by adding an *e*."

He motioned to the hovering waiter. "I think we are ready to order. Angelica?"

"The *salade vinaigrette* and the *ris.*"

"Excellent choice," the waiter murmured. "And for *monsieur?*"

Bedford rattled off his order. "Now then," he began when they were alone again, "Do we put the little transgression in the condo behind us? Or do we see how things progress? I have to say," he added with a wolfish smile, "I did enjoy our kiss."

"It was totally inappropriate," Angelica stammered. "Of course, I take part of the blame."

"Most gracious of you, but it was I who took advantage, and for that I apologize. Cheers," he said, raising his glass.

"*Santé*," Angelica chimed, exalted that she recalled the French toast.

By the time the entrées arrived, she and Bedford were chatting away, their tongues loosened by several glasses of crisp white wine.

"*Madame*," the waiter uttered, "*le ris de veau!*" As triumphant as a magician producing flowers out of thin air, he set down the platter, which consisted of an intricate arrangement of spring vegetables and potato swirls, and—on closer inspection—what appeared to be small testicles swimming in sauce. So much for risotto. Too late, she remembered rice was *riz* with a "z".

"You know," Bedford said smiling as the sommelier refilled her glass, "I made a bet to myself that you would order the chicken. Never took you for a sweetbread kind of girl." He chuckled. "Sounds a lot better than veal's glands, doesn't it?"

Oblivious to her shock, he attacked his own plate with gusto. The tables around them resonated with the hum of voices and clink of silverware on porcelain. It all began to sound rather far away. Bedford, too, seemed to be talking to her from a great distance. She decided not to have any more wine, pretending to sip while her dinner partner regaled her with anecdotes of his years with Northern Atlantic. He recounted how a flight attendant, upon delivering first class food trays to the cockpit crew, had dumped Bedford's all over his head for having stood her up the night before. Angelica suppressed a giggle, thinking it served him right.

"Fortunately, I had a clean shirt in my overnight bag," he went on. "But the co-pilot was laughing so hard he spilt burning hot coffee in his lap. We had to remove his trousers and douse him with the fire extinguisher! But don't worry, you'll never have to fly with me. The FAA revoked my license."

"Really? Why?"

"I wanted to see what would happen if I put a Boeing 737 in reverse in mid-air. There weren't any passengers on board, just a skeleton crew, who weren't too happy about it. In any case, I was through with bussing people around at antisocial hours and doing all those bloody flight checks."

"You put a plane in reverse?" Clearly, the man was certifiable. "I don't think I've ever seen that."

She began to wonder if he would ever broach the subject of his millionaire colleague. They had talked about everything, just about, except the pet food mogul. Finally, after chocolate-drizzled *crème brûlée* and coffee, she explained she had an eight o'clock sales meeting in the morning and had to get going.

Bedford signaled for the check. "See, our dinner date wasn't so terrible, was it? No reason not to mix business with pleasure, don't you think?"

"Actually, now that you mention it, we were going to discuss your colleague. The one who's looking for a beachfront property?"

"Oh, a bit of a SNAFU there, I'm afraid."

"What do you mean?" Angelica asked.

"Can't really talk about it just yet."

Checking her irritation, she smiled politely and rose from the table. "Well, dinner was lovely. Thank you."

He insisted on escorting her back to her car. Standing by the driver's-side door, she held out her hand.

"Goodnight," she said.

Bedford held on to her hand for a moment longer than necessary. "Until next time," he murmured as a camera clicked at the far end of the parking lot.

*****

Beep. "Mayn, this is Bella. I'm trying to get hold of Peter. He's not answering his cell. The Realtor called to say she's holding an open house at the condo on Sunday and wants some of the collectibles stored. Can you have him call me by ten tonight if you get this message?"

Peter listened through to the end, trying to gauge his wife's level of suspicion by the tone of her voice. He visualized her in the Manhattan studio dialing from the Belgian antique phone on the new rococo end table, spending as she was these days like there was no tomorrow. He knew she did it to spite him.

Bella would have known he could not have been dining with Maynard or he'd have had his cell phone switched on. And, clearly, he hadn't been at Maynard's house. He would have to think up an excuse, and fast, but he was good at that. He checked his watch: almost midnight. Too late to call his wife now. He had met up with Lindy at the condo after dinner with Angelica Lane, who had cried off about a meeting in the morning. Usually, he met with less resistance. Her seriousness and modesty appealed to him—a refreshing change from Lindy's petulant wiles and clinging ways.

He'd win the little tease over eventually. It couldn't be that he was losing his touch.

10

93.7 FM's Lite Favorites bounced off the walls in reception, drowning out Angelica's words to everyone but Kathy as she leaned over the front desk, which proudly displayed a photo of the office manager's children and new baby grand-daughter.

Kathy tut-tutted. "And after I warned you not to have dinner with him! Did he, you know, come onto you?"

"Shhh!" Angelica hissed. "Not so much as a kiss. But no more about his rich colleague either."

"Seems you're not going to get one without the other. Oh, by the way, the Peyntons called just now." Kathy held out two slips of paper. "They've decided against any of the homes you showed them yesterday. Dick wondered if you could locate others, with garages unsuitable for 'inhuman habitation,' as he put it, and to call if you find anything. And Mrs. Peynton called separately. She doesn't care about a garage, but a spacious guest suite is essential. Apparently her mother is quite large."

Angelica sighed in frustration, even though the fact that the Peyntons had failed to reconcile their differences came as no real surprise. Obviously, bigger issues were at work than deciding on a floor plan.

"And your dad phoned again," Kathy said, frowning as she glanced at the wall clock. "He must be a night owl out there in Hawaii. Or else an early riser. He said he'd wait up for your call. Hopefully, the meeting won't drag on too long."

Angelica gave Kathy a pained look because they both knew it would. Broker Bob's weekly meetings were legendary.

The office manager handed her a large plate of homemade brownies, which helped promote attendance at these tedious events. The other sales associates were already filing into the conference room. Since Broker Bob had the unfortunate habit of spitting when he got excited, the agents tended to arrive early and jockey for the chairs furthest away from the head of the table. As soon as Angelica deposited the brownies, a flock of hands descended upon them.

"This is the only reason I come to these brutal meetings," Patti mumbled. "I'd rather watch my nails grow."

Angelica took a chair beside Jenn, who was almost her age and wore her hair in a similar style. A Stein Mart navy skirt-suit hung from her bony frame, its dark color accentuating the pallor of her skin. For weeks now, Jenn had declined her invitations to lunch, and Angelica began to suspect the new agent was on a tight budget, even though she certainly worked hard enough. Phil, a tall two-time divorcé in his late forties, sporting a closely shaved door knocker mustache, caught Angelica's gaze and winked. Everyone liked Phil.

Across the table, Gloria sat teasing scarlet-tipped fingers through layers of improbable blond hair. "But the picture on the website doesn't do it justice," she told the person on the other end of her cell phone. "The house is just *darling*. Believe me, it won't last."

Just as a flurry of phones let out a cacophonic fanfare, Rick swaggered into the room, all business and self-importance in his crisp Italian suit. He found a space at the oval table and flipped open his laptop. Bob Plum entered last, trim and dapper in a pale lime shirt accessorized with red silk suspenders and a matching bow tie. The chatter stopped, phones snapped shut.

"Good morning," he greeted the group in nasal tones as, peering through gold-rimmed spectacles, he checked attendance around the table. "Nine," he twanged. "We're missing someone."

"Tyler," Rick offered helpfully. Through the glass wall behind Broker Bob's head, a young agent pulled a face and moved on his way.

Broker Bob smoothed back what was left of his receding gray hair. "We-ell, as independent contractors, I can't force any of you to attend these meetings. However, it is interesting to note that it's always the low producers that seem to miss 'em."

The associates stared at their legal pads, all except Rick who smirked, exempt as he was from Broker Bob's wrath and ridicule.

"We're at month end," Broker Bob droned on, tapping a spreadsheet with an anemic digit. "We made quota, just barely, thanks once again to Rick, but Angelica brought in the biggest listing of the month, with Bedford."

A few words of congratulation circled the table, much to her gratification.

"Now, as you know, folks, our friendly competition for Bill Bungle's office ends when he officially retires next month."

Upon hearing this, the agents grinned, since it was well known that old Bill had unofficially retired two years ago when he made his last sale.

"Which means the associate with the highest revenue for the year by midnight of Thanksgiving Day, to include any executed contract, will take over his office."

Rick and Angelica challenged each other with a brief, hard stare.

Broker Bob went on to deliver a soliloquy on proper disclosures, signage, and other boring minutiae they had all heard before. Meanwhile Angelica drew up the week's shopping list on her pad and made a sketch of a balding man with a beak and a big bowtie. She was just dreaming up a suitable Broker Bob caption that Kathy might find amusing when Frederick Schnauzer, a.k.a. Vodka Fred, proceeded to nod off on her left. A pouchy-eyed, heavy-jowled agent with a paunch, he specialized in commercial real estate. She gave him a warning prod under the table. He awoke with a start, staying alert for a second before slowly slipping back into a stupefied doze. The rest of the agents gazed glassy-eyed into the middle distance or else pretended to take notes on their laptops, continuing to blithely click away beyond the point Broker Bob finally stopped talking. By this time, Fred had sunk into a deep and impenetrable slumber. A prod proving insufficient to stir him this time, Angelica resorted to a shake as soon as Broker Bob turned away to upbraid Tyler for missing the meeting.

She dashed to her desk to return her father's call. "Dad! How are you?" she squealed.

"Just great, Princess. When can I expect a visit?"

It felt so good to hear his mellow voice. "I wish I could've gotten over this summer, but you know how it is in this business. So. What's up?"

"The usual. Catching big waves."

"You still surf?"

"What else would I do on Kauai? This is the place, man."

Angelica smiled to herself, torn between indulgence and concern. "Okay, but watch out for tiger sharks." Too late, she realized she sounded just like her mother.

"How *is* your mother?" her father asked.

"Busy getting the new house ready. I may be going to Oregon for Christmas."

"That's nice," her father said, but Angelica sensed his disappointment. "Look," he said after a pause, "It's just that, well, there's someone special I'd like you to meet. Her name is Nuala."

Angelica stiffened in her chair. How could her mother be twice wed and her dad have a significant other when she had not walked down the aisle one single time, and all she'd ever had were *insignificant* others? Even her sister, four years her junior, had a steady relationship.

"She's an elementary school teacher in Hanalei," her father added.

The light on Angelica's phone blinked. "That's wonderful, Dad. Listen, I'll see what I can do about getting time off, okay? I'll call soon, I promise."

Painfully aware that her conversations with her father were always too short, she hung up, realizing she had not even had time to ask about Claire whose voice mail she kept getting. Her phone flashed impatiently.

"Finally!" Kathy's voice rushed down the line. "Someone called about listing their house. You were next on rotation. Swing by my desk for the details. I set you up for a one-thirty."

Angelica checked her watch. She would have plenty of time to run off a stack of "comps" beforehand. If she gave as good a presentation as she had for Bella Bedford she might acquire this other listing as well, and get a rung up on Rick.

11

*T*he blacktop dead-ended in a cul-de-sac, beyond which stretched raw acres of slash pine and sabal palm. Angelica pulled over by the side of the road and consulted the map. Inexplicably lost, she began to panic.

When at one-thirty she finally phoned the homeowner for directions, a three-tone signal assaulted her ear. The ensuing recording stated the number was no longer in service. She called the office. "Kathy, I can't find Ms. Fioretti's address and the number's been disconnected!"

"I made her repeat it. She said it was a new subdivision, but if you kept going east on Palmetto, you couldn't miss the sign."

"There is no sign. Oh, well, perhaps she'll call again." But somehow Angelica knew she wouldn't. It had to have been a bogus call. But why?

Different scenarios, most of them featuring Rick, played in her head as she drove back to the office where Broker Bob accosted her in reception.

"Back from your listing appointment so soon?" he trilled.

"I couldn't find it."

"You couldn't *what?*"

"No such address, no such phone number."

Broker Bob frowned prissily. "You mean to say you went all the way out to the boonies without confirming the appointment beforehand?"

"Kathy made the appointment only this morning," Angelica told him.

He yanked a paper cone from the cooler and squirted water into it, raising his voice. "Perhaps Kathy didn't hear correctly because the music in here is so unbelievably loud."

Kathy set the volume to a more believable level.

"Now, about those buyers of yours," he began.

"The Peyntons?"

"What is their status?"

"They're in a holding pattern," Angelica said, keeping the dialogue technical and discussing her clients as though they were a pair of hovering airplanes. "They have marital issues."

"You must counsel these people," Broker Bob lectured. "Help define their needs and overturn their objections. Win their confidence and you will make friends for life!"

Angelica was aghast at the thought.

"Now!" Broker Bob said. "Is there not *something* you can do?"

"Not really, short of assassinating the mother-in-law in Cleveland. And I'm sure Dick Peynton already thought of that."

"Well, keep working on it," Broker Bob exhorted before stalking off in the direction of his office.

With a roll of her eyes, Angelica proceeded to the reception desk.

"I took down the address carefully," Kathy assured her.

"I'm sure you did. A wrong address *and* phone number is just too much of a coincidence."

Angelica tried to shrug off the incident as she perused her message slips, but doubts lingered at the back of her mind. Who had the most to gain from wasting her time? That was an easy one: Rick Powers. She voiced her suspicions to Kathy.

"Could equally well be Gloria," the office manager said.

"Really? Why?"

"She's jealous of you."

"She is? But why?"

"Because you're independent, successful, and naturally attractive."

"I am? I'm not as together as you think, you know. It's a persona I slip into at work. Underneath I always wonder if I'm perfect enough."

"Who expects you to be perfect?"

"My mother. She was always criticizing everything I did. When my parents divorced, I thought it was all my fault."

"Listen, Angelica, you've got to stop beating yourself up. Your mother might be wrong, have you ever considered that? Now get back to work," the office manager said with mock sternness. "And, remember, you're your own woman."

"Yes, ma'am. I'll be in my cubicle if you think of any other suspects."

Dropping her briefcase on the floor, Angelica slumped into the swivel chair at her desk. The Fioretti listing appointment was a major disappointment. If she didn't write another contract by Thanksgiving, she could kiss Bill Bungle's office goodbye. Oh, but she couldn't bear the idea of Rick getting the office!

As if her thoughts had conjured him up in person, he appeared at the opening to her cubicle. "Angelica, I overheard what you said about the Peyntons. Tough deal, kiddo."

Angelica looked up, sighing in irritation as he scooted onto a corner of her desk and leaned over to pat her knee. "Thanks," she said starchily, wheeling herself out of reach. "But, if you don't mind, I just want to be alone."

He raised his palms. "Whoa, Garbo! I just came to commiserate, is all." And humming cheerfully, he moved off her desk and made for the exit.

"Honk," she mouthed after him, louder than intended.

His head spun around. "What was that?"

"Did you hear about the wild goose chase I went on?"

He looked baffled. And innocent.

"So you didn't hear the reprimand I got from Broker Bob?"

"No."

"Failure to confirm a listing appointment ahead of time."

Rick puckered his perfectly proportioned nose. "Don't sweat it. He's in a bad mood because his biotech stocks took a tumble. Better to invest in Florida real estate, ha! Safe as houses, and all that bull."

"Okay, thanks," she murmured, backing down. Rick *seemed* sincere, anyway. Or else he was a consummate actor.

The moment he left, she closed her eyes, reviewing her morning. She couldn't get the Peyntons what they each wanted for the amount they could afford to pay. To think of all the research and legwork she had put in on their behalf! On top of that, she had wasted time on an abortive listing appointment and gotten chewed out by Broker Bob. And, as if all *that* wasn't enough, her entanglement with Peter Bedford was a lose-lose situation.

Her only hope was to get the Plovers Key condo sold soon.

12

*A*t five o'clock on Sunday, Angelica showed the last visitors out of the Bedfords' condo. Kathy had supplied gingerbread cookies for the event, and these had gone down a treat. All in all, it had been a successful open house with at least three A-list prospects. In addition, she had registered a handful of new customers looking for property in the higher-end market.

Congratulating herself on a job well done, she sat on the sofa putting away her papers. Just as she was closing her briefcase, a knock rapped on the front door, and Peter Bedford sauntered into the living room, his white shorts and T-shirt accentuating a ruddy tan.

"Hmm, smells good in here," he declared with his customary bluster.

"Cinnamon pot-pourri," Angelica informed him.

"Good idea. Very welcoming."

Angelica felt less than welcoming in his regard, but at least he had noticed her efforts.

"I was out on my boat cruising around Sanibel and thought I'd pop in to see how the open house went."

"I think we'll get some calls," she said confidently, to prove his wife had made the right choice in selecting her to list the property.

"Good. Mineral water?" Bedford called from the kitchen.

Angelica searched around for her cell phone. "Thanks, but

I was just getting ready to leave."

He prowled back into the room. "You're always running away, aren't you, Angelica?" He upended the plastic bottle of Evian into his mouth. "Most women don't find me so undesirable," he said after quenching his thirst.

"I know," she said evenly.

He approached her, his expression one of amused curiosity. "You *know?*"

"I mean . . . Oh, never mind." She fastened down the catches on her briefcase.

"On the contrary, please continue." He deposited the water on the coffee table and crossed his arms as though he had all the time in the world.

"Well, if you really want to know, I walked in here the other week and saw you in bed with someone," she said in a heated rush.

"Ah." Bedford smiled bashfully. "That woman was—"

Angelica raised a hand to ward off his confidences. "You certainly don't have to explain yourself to me. And, of course, I wouldn't dream of mentioning it to your wife." Tucking her jacket under her arm, she reached for her briefcase.

Bedford seized both briefcase and jacket and tossed them into an armchair. "Wait just a minute, will you."

The air hummed with electricity as he stepped toward her, jaw thrust forward, the gold specks in his eyes throwing off sparks. Taking her by the shoulders, he propelled her backward until her calves touched the sofa.

"Angelica," he growled.

His lips descended upon hers, devouring her mouth. She could taste the sun and salt on him. She felt her will siphoning out of her body. Her resistance bid her body farewell, leaving her limp in his embrace. He forced her against the sofa, and her knees gave way. The next second, he was on top of her, nibbling her ear. "There is something so clean and proper about you," he whispered hoarsely. "It makes me want to defile you."

Angelica gasped. His tongue traced the hollow at the base of her throat. His hands dug into the seat cushions and cupped her bottom, pulling her up against him, his breath coming quick and hard against her neck. A swooning sensation swept through her. Dear God, she thought, I'm about to be *defiled!*

From somewhere deep within her, she realized she must on no account become Peter Bedford's next conquest. His hazel eyes held an animal hunger, the mocking look of a lion that had just caught his prey. Snapping out of her swoon, she sat up on her elbows and pulled herself onto the arm of the sofa, noting with satisfaction his expression of surprise.

"Very well," he muttered, adding sarcastically, "I suppose you best be going now."

Angelica straightened her clothes, and without so much as a glance or goodbye, grabbed her belongings and left. Too impatient to wait for an elevator, she barreled down the fire stairs, almost colliding with a man in dark sunglasses. A rush of warm air hit her as she exited the building. She hurried to her car.

"It's not my fault," she told herself, but judging by the controlled tone of Bedford's voice, it seemed he thought otherwise. He might as well have called her a tease.

Scalded by anger, she drove home in a daze. Back at her condo, she threw on a leotard and the woolen leg warmers she had kept since her early teens, before she'd gotten too tall to entertain any serious dreams of becoming a ballerina. Upon lacing up her sneakers, she led Hercules to the poolside gym and stood him on a treadmill set at a slow pace.

A step machine, elliptical cross-trainer and a second treadmill took up the rest of the central floor place facing the wall-to-wall mirror, where a rack of weights, rolled-up yoga mats, and a pair of inflatable colored balls lay in a row.

Adjusting the controls on her machine, she began to walk, building up to a fast clip and reflecting that, after she limbered up, she might try a few of the other instruments of torture arranged around the room: the Leg-Crunch or Butt-Blaster perhaps. Her heartbeat quickened, the blood pumped through her veins. As the machine sped up, she broke into a jog, pounding away the embarrassing encounter with Peter Bedford and cursing him with every breath.

Before long, the Lycra began to stick to her body, a film of perspiration coated her face. She was running hard now, she felt mad at the world! Taking deep breaths, she settled into a rhythm. She could run like this forever. On and on she ran. This must be her record on the treadmill. Suddenly she heard a squeak above the purr of machines.

Hercules!

Spotting a blur of stubby legs, she leaped to his rescue. His treadmill had automatically picked up speed. "Oh!" she gasped, snatching him from the conveyor belt. "I didn't mean for you to get that much exercise!" Panting, he crumpled to the floor, the pale blue bow askew on his head. "Herx! Herx!" she coaxed, wondering if she should attempt mouth-to-snout resuscitation.

She rushed to the mini fridge and grabbed a bottle of water, tipping a trickle over the dog's mouth. He blinked open his eyes and let out a feeble sigh. Angelica gathered him up in her arms and carried him home. Her thigh muscles throbbed. She could only imagine how poor Hercules felt. It was all Bedford's fault. Why couldn't he have returned to Manhattan with his wife and left her to get on with the sale of the condo unmolested?

Making her way along the path in the dark, she could not rid herself of the feeling that Bedford would not take this latest rejection lying down. He had seemed very put out.

*****

Peering from the foliage, the spy watched Angelica's every move. She looked hot. Literally. The leotard clung to her like a peel-off pore strip. The dog was in a lather as well and appeared half dead. What had she been doing? Using it as a dumbbell? The mini waterfall drowned out his laughter as his subject passed close by with her pet. Still, he reflected more seriously, she should pay more attention when she went out alone at night. You never knew who might be lurking about. Just witness all the abductions of young women featured on the news these days. Seemed like every week, one more disappeared.

13

*D*uring the week, Angelica conducted two showings of her listing in Palm Meadow, a small but well-maintained town house located close to schools and shopping, ideal for a young family. Her two-line ad in the paper had elicited half a dozen calls in two days, but still no word from anyone who had been to the Sunday open house at Plovers Key. She had felt sure there would be some follow-up on the property, which was being sold turnkey and offered such breathtaking views. She could not understand it.

"That listing is jinxed," she told Kathy over the *whump-thud* of the office photo copier.

"You've only had it two weeks, hon."

"I know, but it's such a sweet deal, even in this market."

If she sold Plovers Key along with the Palm Meadow property, she stood a good chance of beating Rick in the contest for Bill's coveted office. A big "if" at this point. All of a sudden, Jenn rushed toward them, mousy hair flying around her pale face.

"Angelica, have you seen your car?" the young agent blurted, grabbing her arm and dragging her toward the lobby.

"What d'you mean?"

"Someone keyed it."

Angelica tore into the parking lot and drew a sharp breath when she saw the passenger side of her car, the word B-I-T-C-H etched in the glossy white paintwork, two of the letters scraped down to the metal.

"When could it have happened?" Kathy asked behind her, appraising the damage.

Angelica mentally revisited the places she had been that day. "After Palm Meadow, I went to the carwash. I would have noticed it then, so it must have happened here."

She had meant to stop only briefly at the office and hadn't bothered to lock her car, otherwise she might have heard the alarm. Gazing around the parking lot, she saw that only her vehicle appeared to have been singled out for abuse.

"Are you going to report it to Broker Bob?" Kathy asked.

"He'll just say my car was in a public lot and absolve Plum Realty from any responsibility. I have a high deductible. It wouldn't be worth filing a claim."

"Well, you can't go around advertising yourself as a bitch," Kathy said sensibly.

"I suppose I could get a rental car until the paintwork is fixed."

"We'd better warn the office. And you should call the police." Kathy pointed to the scrapes. "This wasn't a random act. It was a vicious attack."

"Where's Rick today?"

Kathy shot her a glance. "Why do you ask?"

"I'm wondering who might have it in for me. Rick's got the best motive. He'd do anything to hurt my chances in the contest for Bill's office. And what about that bogus appointment I went on? He could have put one of his friends up to that."

"Listen, hon," Kathy reasoned, removing her eyeglasses and cleaning them on the cuff of her blouse. "Rick's got his faults, but he wouldn't do something like this."

"I brushed him off the other day," Angelica insisted. "Maybe that's what sparked this off."

"We could have a handwriting expert check it out. Rick's

left-handed. But it looks more like a woman's work."

"The graffiti would have to be compared to a handwriting sample," Angelica said. "If it's someone outside the office, we'd be none the wiser."

"True. I wonder if the police could take prints. It'd be great if you had just waxed your car."

"I didn't. Just a regular wash and the spot-free rinse. I don't see any prints."

The rest of the afternoon passed anxiously as Angelica contended with this latest problem. She decided not to involve the police. Broker Bob would throw a fit if the cops turned up at his premises. Nor did she have to tell anyone at work to be on the alert for a graffiti artist, as Jenn had already broadcast the news. Rick came to her to express his concern after first repositioning his car so he could keep an eye on it from his window.

"Someone's got it in for you," he said, stressing the "someone."

Angelica agreed. "But who?"

Could it be Rick? Who else could it be? The question tortured her for the rest of the day.

That evening she called her sister's number and left another message. "Claire, it's me. I'm worried about you. Let me know you're okay. Please. I spoke to dad. Did he tell you about Nuala? Mom's fine. I'm fine. Well, not really. There's some weird stuff going on at work."

In fact, a lot seemed to be going wrong since Peter Bedford entered her life. Or, more accurately, since she had walked in on his. She began to wish she had never landed the listing.

14

Internal Memo
To: Angelica
From: Kathy
Re: Handwriting Analysis

From what I could dig up on the Internet, the culprit is probably right-handed, vain and materialistic (flourish on "B"), selfish (leftward tendency on "I"), very emotional (overly right slant on most letters), and possibly unstable (variable slants). Pressure level and spiky strokes demonstrate intensity of emotion (watch out!!). Gender of person inconclusive. To compare and contrast, I took a sample of Broker Bob's writing and, wouldn't you know it: all introspective, anal left slants.

With a snicker of amusement, Angelica made her way to the front desk to discuss the findings with Kathy. "Thanks for going to all that trouble," she said. "So I'm dealing with a psycho, by the sound of it."

"Could be. Analyzing handwriting is quite interesting. I traced the letters, and then took the sheet home to research. I don't know how much help it'll be."

"Well, it does give a profile of the—" Angelica broke off. "Don't look now," she muttered. "Broker Bob's headed over here. Looks like he's on the war path."

"How did this memo get on my desk?" he demanded, holding out a sheet of paper, which Angelica recognized as Kathy's memo.

"Oh, shoot," Kathy said under her breath. "I have no idea," she told Broker Bob. "Someone must have made a copy."

"So it's not some kind of joke?"

"Handwriting analysis is a hobby of mine. I was helping Angelica find out who keyed her car."

"I see. And how did my name get into your *private* little memo?"

"I was simply trying to prove that the person who keyed her car was not a rational person like yourself," Kathy said with absolute cool.

Angelica was unequal to the task of keeping her face straight. A giggle escaped her, which she unsuccessfully tried to disguise as a cough.

Broker Bob thrust the memo into Kathy's hand. "I believe one of the adjectives used to describe me was 'anal.' "

"That's short-form for analytical," Kathy explained.

"Perhaps if the two of you spent less time gossiping and more time concentrating on your jobs, there'd be fewer mix-ups with appointments," Broker Bob said pointedly. "And Angelica would be less distracted about locking her car. Shred every copy of this," he commanded before storming off to his office.

Angelica turned to Kathy. "Who do you think made a copy?"

"Well, let's see," Kathy said, checking her list of which agents had been on the premises that day. "Old Bill Bungle could've gotten confused, I suppose, and wandered into your cubicle. But I don't think he knows how to work the copier." She held Broker Bob's copy up to the light and then to her nose. "It was Gloria."

"How do you know?" Angelica asked in surprise.

"It's her perfume. Faint but distinct enough."

Angelica took a whiff. "Maybe."

"Believe me. I sit here all day. I can tell one perfume and aftershave from another. Plus I'm allergic to one of the ingredients in Witchy Woman. It always makes me sneeze."

"Should we confront her about it?"

"I've got a better idea." Kathy grabbed a black marker and added a smiley face on the bottom of the memo. "I'm going to leave this on her desk. If it wasn't Gloria who snitched on us, she'll come looking for an explanation."

"Didn't Broker Bob tell us to shred every copy of the memo?" Angelica asked.

"Yes, but he didn't specify when."

The office manager went to place the sheet on Gloria's desk. The agent had left. The afternoon passed. Gloria finally came, and went again. She said nothing about the memo.

"Can't say I'm surprised," Kathy commented as she and Angelica stood beside the damaged car before parting for home. "But I don't think Gloria is guilty of vandalism. The perpetrator would hardly want to draw attention to herself or himself by copying the memo."

Angelica's response was interrupted by the phone ringing in her jacket pocket.

"Hello, Angelica," an elderly male voice warbled in her ear. "Dr. Epstein here. I met you at the open house at Plovers Key Tower on Sunday."

Angelica darted a hopeful look at Kathy. "Yes, Dr. Epstein. How are you?"

"Dandy, thank you. My wife and I would like to take another look at the condominium, if we may."

Angelica nodded excitedly at Kathy while the doctor spoke. She recalled the retired couple who had partaken of the gingerbread cookies and coffee, and who had spent a good half hour going through the rooms. "Yes, tomorrow morning would be fine," she said. "Nine-thirty is perfect."

"Any chance we could meet the owner?"

"Unfortunately, Mrs. Bedford is out of town," Angelica stalled, desperate not to involve her husband.

"I know it's not strictly necessary," the old doctor said, "but Isabel and I would feel more comfortable if we knew the people who are selling the condominium. We're a bit old-fashioned that way."

Angelica felt she had no choice but to comply. "I understand. Well, Mrs. Bedford arranged the listing, but I can see if her husband is available." Hopefully, he wouldn't be.

After the call, Angelica explained the situation to Kathy, omitting the incident with Bedford on the sofa, an incident she had tried unsuccessfully to banish from her mind. But, as usual, Kathy's intuition honed in on the crux of the matter.

"At least you won't be alone with him," she said. "Oh, hon, let's hope you can just close on the condo and move on, and put this one down to experience."

"Fingers crossed," Angelica murmured, thinking if she sold Plovers Key, she could afford to buy a new car—although that didn't solve the problem of who hated her enough to deface her vehicle in the first place. Probably the same person who had sent her to the non-existent property in the middle of nowhere.

But why?

15

*T*hat evening, Angelica sorted through the contents of her briefcase, checking that her pens and calculator worked and were stored in their proper compartments for ease of access, in the event the Epsteins made an offer. Best to avoid looking inept when helping people part with a large chunk of money, she always thought. She reread the condo documents and called Mrs. Bedford to give her a progress report, informing her that her husband would be attending the meeting with the prospects the next day.

"That's wonderful news," Bella enthused in honeysuckle inflections. "I'm glad Peter has been helpful."

"Oh, yes," Angelica lied, wondering, not for the first time, if Mrs. Bedford had the slightest clue about her husband's predatory ways.

"You are such a doll! You think the Epsteins will buy?"

"We'll see," Angelica answered, not wishing to give rise to false hope. "But they seem like serious prospects." She had been in real estate long enough to peg a looky-loo when she saw one.

That night, she went to bed early with a new romantic suspense novel Jenn had recommended. "Have a box of tissues handy," her colleague had advised.

Hoping to distract herself from the next day's meeting, Angelica settled down to a good read. She so desperately wanted to bring the whole business of the Plovers Key condo to a close that she felt something might go wrong at the last minute. So much had gone wrong already.

She refused to let herself think of that now.

The bedside clock ticked away the next hour and a quarter while she lost track of time and place, transported as she was to the home of the handsome, enigmatic hero. The stalker was out there somewhere, and Eleanor was alone . . .

"The dark presence of someone standing beside the bed wrested her from sleep. Or was she still dreaming? Eleanor could not move. Double gravity weighed down her limbs. Nor could she scream. She struggled for full consciousness, for a voice.

'Angel!' she gasped, staring up at the man's shadow.

He bent toward her. It was over for her now, she knew. Angel had found her, and Emile was gone. She shrank back in the bed and let out a strangled scream . . ."

A bark? Hercules' frantic outburst catapulted Angelica out of the pages of her book and off the bed. He didn't usually yap indoors. Finding him scratching at the front door, she checked the lock. She then ran in her bare feet to the kitchen. The lampposts cast an eerie white blur through the blinds. Peeking between them, she saw nothing unusual on the concrete path below.

Guided by the shaft of light from her bedroom, she groped her way to the dining room and pulled her phone off the charger. As the dog's snarling lowered in pitch, she thought she heard the shuffle of footsteps outside, followed by the squeak of the stair rail. Whoever it was had been scared off, thanks to her pet.

Alarming thoughts rattled around in her head. Were the car vandal and the late night intruder one and the same person? Or were the two incidents coincidental? A few homeless people lived in the nearby woods. It was easy enough to climb over the wall surrounding the community. She wondered whom she could turn to for help, her only permanent neighbor being a doddery old widower with a passion for origami. Most of the other residents wintered at the Cascades and would not start arriving for a few weeks.

She was virtually alone. And frightened—like the heroine in Jenn's novel. That's what happened when you read thrillers late at night, Angelica scolded herself. She had an important meeting with prospects the next day and could not afford to lose her composure. Too much was at stake.

16

"You look pale," Kathy noted with a concerned frown the following morning as she stapled sheaves of paper together. Broker Bob had no compunction about sacrificing trees to the cause of real estate and enjoyed keeping the Realtors' trays loaded with material that usually got recycled without being read.

"I had a scare last night. Nothing to worry about, probably," Angelica said with more conviction than she felt. "But I'll have to tell you about it later—I'm meeting with the Epsteins in an hour at Plovers Key. Do we have a blank sales agreement?"

Kathy reached into a file cabinet behind her desk and pulled a Fla-Bar sales contract from a hanging folder. "Here, hon, take this one. I'll print up some more."

"Thanks." Angelica snatched a pen from the desk. "What's the date today?"

"November fifth."

Angelica dated the contract and slid the form in her briefcase.

"By the way, a gift came for you," Kathy said. "It's on your desk."

Angelica perked up at the news. "Really? Who's it from?"

"Haven't a clue. Looks pretty, though. I found it on my desk with a note saying, '*For Angelica.*' "

Puzzled, Angelica made for her cubicle. Could it be she

had a secret admirer? Or perhaps it was a token of appreciation from a satisfied customer. She had received cookies and bath accessories in the past, even a crate of pears. With a quiver of anticipation, she entered her workspace and beheld a box on her desk wrapped in silver paper and topped with a festive orange bow. She picked up the gift, which was quite light. Definitely not bubble bath or foot massage lotion, she concluded.

Jenn, passing by with a mug of steaming coffee, asked if she was going to open it.

Angelica hesitated. "I thought I'd wait until I got home."

"You think it might be some naughty lingerie?" Jenn lowered her voice as she leaned against the partition wall, cradling her mug. "Ooh, how exciting! Please open it," she begged. "I swear I won't tell."

Angelica shot her a conspiratorial grin. "Oh, alright then. The suspense is killing me too."

The only other people she could imagine sending her a gift were her family, but this box had not come in the mail. She searched for a card and, finding none, peeled off the bow and removed the decorative paper. Beneath, she found a plain green cardboard box. She popped open the lid, and *BOOM!*

As the gift exploded, someone in the office screamed, and Jenn's mug hit the floor. Silver stars attached to red and yellow streamers erupted into the air. Smoke billowed toward the ceiling.

Broker Bob flew out of his office, mopping his pale domed brow with a red silk handkerchief. "Wha-what happened?" he shrilled, competing in pitch with the smoke detector alarm. "Is anything damaged? Is anyone hurt? Remember, you can't sue!"

Angelica stood rooted to the floor of her cubicle. Kathy rushed to her side. Once the alarm piped down into protracted squeaks, everybody started talking at once.

"That was no ordinary smoke bomb," croaked Bill Bungle, a veteran of Korea, feebly waving away wisps of smoke.

Broker Bob glared at the multicolor streamers strewn on the carpet. "Will someone please tell me what the dickens is going on here?"

"I opened the box and it exploded," Angelica explained, picking up debris from the floor. " '*Remember, remember the fifth of November,*' " she read aloud from the inside of the lid.

"Well, no one's very likely to forget it now," Broker Bob retorted.

" '*Gunpowder, treason and plot!* ' " she finished quoting from the old English verse.

"What? Who did the box come from?"

Angelica recalled where she had heard the rhyme before. "From Peter Bedford, my Plovers Key client. I think he was just throwing a prank on his birthday."

"I see," Broker Bob said in a tight voice. "Your client has a weird sense of humor."

"He's British."

"Aren't you meeting with a prospect at his condo this morning?"

"Yes, and I best get going." She snatched up her briefcase, glad of the cue to escape. "I'll finish cleaning this up later," she added, gesturing toward the ripped paper and cardboard on the carpet. Not to mention the coffee splatters.

"Just be sure and come back with a signed contract," Broker Bob sputtered before marching back to his office.

Ignoring the curious expressions on her colleagues' faces, and Gloria's gloating one, Angelica flew from the premises. Peter Bedford! What an idiot, she fumed. What was he thinking? She preferred to arrive calm and collected at meetings, not rushed and irate.

Flooring the gas all the way to Plovers Key, she blared her horn at the early snowbirds in their slow-boat Lincolns and Cadillacs, and screeched into the parking space beside Bedford's bronze Aston Martin. The sunroof was open, the sky overcast. Angelica hoped it would rain all over his molded two-tone leather interior.

She strode into the lobby and slammed her fist on the elevator button.

Calm down. This is not the right mindset for closing a sale, she reminded herself, and began practicing deep, slow breathing on the way up to the eighth floor. She smoothed her hair behind her ear and straightened the lapels of her gray jacket. Then, with measured steps, she approached #801 and knocked on the door.

There had better be a good explanation for this, she thought, though for the life of her she could not imagine what that might be.

17

A quick glance around the living room assured Angelica that the Epsteins had not yet arrived. She let out a sigh of relief. Peter Bedford, dressed in dark slacks and a light cashmere sweater in a caramel hue, lounged on the sofa reading the *Wall Street Journal.* His nonchalance irritated her.

" 'We are not amused,' to quote your Queen Victoria," she snapped.

Bedford grinned boyishly. "Ah," he said. "I see you got my little surprise."

Angelica perched on an armchair, her back ramrod straight. "Thanks to your 'little surprise,' an octogenarian agent at my office almost had a heart attack. The smoke alarm went off. My broker thought we were under a terrorist attack. He is *not* pleased."

Peter Bedford failed to look contrite. "He'll forgive you when you bring in the sale, won't he? I only wanted my birthday to go off with a bang. It's Bonfire Night back home. People will be setting off fireworks. Children will be waving their sparklers. I miss this time of year in England," he added wistfully.

Angelica found herself wishing she could burn an effigy of Peter Bedford and join in the celebrations. She exhaled a patient breath. "Please understand. This is my work and it just isn't professional—"

"Angelica, you really need to get over yourself. Given the

choice, I'd have liked us to make fireworks of our own."

"Mr. Bedford!" Really, the man was incorrigible.

He set his newspaper aside. "Fair enough. Perhaps I should not have sent an exploding device to your place of work. Actually, I was planning to leave it on your doorstep so you would find it first thing this morning, but when I heard your dog going bonkers, I was afraid you might see the box and open it before the appropriate time."

Angelica gasped in indignation. "So it was *you* lurking outside my door last night! How did you find out my address?"

"You're in the phone book."

"How did you get through the gate without a code?"

"I vaulted over it. Anyway, what does it matter?"

"What does it matter?" Angelica erupted. "I was up most of the night, terrified someone was trying to break in."

"How like you to overreact."

"Overreact? Someone trashed my car! Was that one of your silly pranks too?"

"Really, Miss Lane, let's not get hysterical, not to mention paranoid."

Angelica could have sworn he stressed the word "Miss." She narrowed her eyes at him, fingers clawing with the urge to scratch his face to shreds. "Not get *hysterical?*" she hissed. "I cannot believe what I'm hearing!"

Peter Bedford frowned. "I'm sorry you didn't appreciate my little joke, but I assure you I did *not* touch your car. I have the utmost respect for people's cars. If anyone laid hands on my Astie, I'd bloody throttle them."

He looked most indignant. Angelica hesitated for a moment, and finally sighed in resignation. Right now, more was at stake than who had done what, she decided. The important thing was to make the sale and terminate all contact with Peter Bedford at the earliest opportunity.

"Very well then. Apology accepted." She glanced at her watch. "I'd better give you the lowdown on the Epsteins before they arrive. They're from Rochester, New York. They're in their seventies and really sweet."

She fluffed up an armchair cushion and scanned the room to make sure everything was in order. But for Bedford's stupid stunt, she would have had time to pick up a bouquet of fresh flowers for the dining room table.

"Sweet? Unlike me, you mean." Bedford smiled his wolfish smile.

"Yes, no! I mean you'll like them. And I'm sure they'll be punctual." The doorbell rang. "See?"

Angelica went to welcome the Epsteins into the condo. After first establishing her level of representation in their regard, as required by her profession, she made the introductions. The hand the old doctor extended to Bedford was speckled with liver spots, his wrist knotty and gnarled. He wore his brown pants pulled up to his midsection, and yet still managed to maintain an air of dignity about him. His snowy-haired wife, petite and spry in a pale blue smock blouse and matching slacks, carried an old-fashioned purse in the crook of her arm.

"Call me Isabel," she insisted.

Angelica congratulated herself on having produced such delightful and respectable buyers.

Bedford, looking particularly robust in contrast, played the jovial host. The Epsteins appeared to lap up his earnest enthusiasm and well-bred British accent, which Angelica felt sure he exaggerated for their benefit as he listed all the amenities to be enjoyed at Plovers Key: the pristine state park on their doorstep, the beach, pool, and below-ground hot tub. He was sorry to be giving up the location and views, he told them, but he missed his homeland. Dr. Epstein and his wife nodded in understanding. Angelica invited them to sit down and offered them a drink.

"Oh, you don't need to fuss over us, my dear," Isabel Epstein chirped, flitting around the living room and exclaiming now and then with endearing delight. "John, did you see this shell? Such a pretty salmon pink! Almost the same color as this building."

"We beach-combed that conch in the Bahamas," Bedford explained. "My wife likes to collect dustibles. Angelica stored some of them away for safekeeping, but most are being sold with the condo."

"Just a few pictures and some porcelain figurines," Angelica explained, recalling all the clutter she had lugged to the closet. "Let me show them to you." She led Isabel Epstein into the master bedroom in an attempt to regain control of her clients. Peter Bedford seemed to have taken over the proceedings, and she had to show she was capable of doing her job.

"I'm not sure I'll keep that abstract on the wall," Isabel observed, shaking her white bun. "It sort of has the evil eye."

Angelica gave the picture a cursory glance. "There are a couple of seascapes in here you might like better," she said, opening the wall-to-wall closet.

"Oh, I do like that one of the Baie des Anges. John and I went to Nice for our honeymoon. Many moons ago, of course." Isabel's laughter tinkled in the room as she held up the oil painting against the abstract at the foot of the bed, admiring the effect.

"I'm glad you like it," Angelica said, heartened that Isabel seemed to have made the transition from observer to occupant—always a promising sign. She only hoped that Bedford was behaving himself with the doctor. He was, to say the least, unpredictable, as she had learned to her cost.

"However, I don't much care for the knick-knacks," Isabel admitted, peering into the closet.

"I don't either. That's why I put them in here."

"Then we're in agreement." Laughing, Isabel took Angelica's arm and they strolled back into the living room where the two men stood on the balcony, chatting away like old friends.

"Well, dear," Dr. Epstein asked his wife, "Do you like the condominium as much as before?"

"Oh, I do, John."

"Very well," the doctor said, turning to Bedford. "You're asking nine hundred and ninety-nine thousand dollars. We'd like to propose nine hundred and fifty. Thousand, of course."

This evinced a chuckle from Isabel. Angelica's heart missed a beat as Bedford considered what, to her mind, was a highly satisfactory offer. He looked doubtful. Would he counter? Flat-out refuse? She waited, glancing at her clients, who stared at him in anticipation. She could have kicked him. Just as she felt sure Peter Bedford would make difficulties, he held out his hand to Dr. Epstein.

"Accepted."

Breathing an inward sigh of relief, Angelica congratulated the buyers. "When would you like to close?" she asked.

Isabel clapped her hands together. "In time for the holidays? Oh, John, how wonderful!"

"Now then," the doctor said, addressing Angelica. "I have here a deposit check. We'll be making a cash purchase. If you could write up the contract, we'll take it with us and look it over, if we may. We can overnight the signed agreement to your office this afternoon."

Minutes later, Angelica presided at the head of the dining room table with the Epsteins seated on either side of her. Having written in an addendum for the contents and attached the inventory list, she helped the buyers settle on a title company and a closing date of November twentieth.

Bella Bedford would be thrilled to hear about the quick sale.

"You are going to love it here," Bedford said, showing the Epsteins to the door after they had taken a leisurely stroll around the condo, discussing minor changes they would make to the furnishings.

After the exchange of a few more pleasantries, the buyers left, announcing they were going to make another tour of the communal pool and private beach.

Bedford handed Angelica a manila envelope. "You'd better take this. It contains documents pertaining to the condo. I'm living out of a suitcase in town and chances are I might lose it. Now, how about celebrating? I have a lunch engagement, but we could have dinner tonight."

Angelica smiled, aglow with success and almost ready to agree to anything. "Tell you what. Tomorrow, I'll deliver the sales agreement to you personally for your signature and we can drink to it then."

Peter Bedford held out his hand. "No hard feelings?"

Angelica shook it. "None."

It was true. He had, in all fairness, been instrumental in closing the sale. Besides which, after tomorrow, she would never have to see him again.

Bedford opened the door for her. "You're not such a bad sport after all," he jested, and Angelica laughed as she passed into the corridor.

Still smiling, she waited for the elevator. She would go back to the office and tell Broker Bob about the imminent sale of the condo for almost list price. With no other broker involved, she would get full commission, less Plum Realty's fees. Broker Bob would kiss the ground she walked on. The explosion, the coffee stain on the carpet, everything would be forgiven.

When the doors closed on the elevator car, she let out a whoop of glee. It was really going to happen! Salesperson of the month, reserved parking, Bill's office with her name on the door, and a hefty deposit in her bank account. Unlikely Rick could pull such a big fat bunny out of the hat in the next three weeks.

As she approached her car, having first visited the restroom off the lobby and given her card to a chatty, overstuffed woman in a bikini, Angelica glanced up at the condo tower in time to see a man fall to the parking lot, arms flailing, face taut in the updraft. Red-blond hair trailed above him, resembling a comet.

She watched in disbelief as Peter Bedford plummeted eight floors and crashed through the open sunroof of his Aston Martin.

18

*T*he car rocked with the impact, the alarm began bleating. The Epsteins appeared out of nowhere, the doctor motioning to his wife to stay put near the corner of the building as he executed a fast hobble to where Bedford sprawled half in, half out of the bronze Aston Martin.

"Call nine-one-one," he directed Angelica. And then, as he took hold of Peter's wrist, "Tell them he's dead."

The thump of Bedford's body had brought a handful of rubbernecks from the private fringe of beach, but there proved little to see with Angelica's vehicle parked in front of the sports car, and politely waved away by the old doctor, they drifted back to their lounge chairs.

Dr. Epstein rested a frail hand on Angelica's shoulder. "Nothing to be done, dear. Broken neck. A coroner's report will most likely confirm that Mr. Bedford died instantaneously upon impact."

Isabel joined them, clutching a white lace handkerchief to her mouth. "Such a nice young man too. I wonder what could have happened?"

Angelica followed the doctor's gaze to the eighth floor, where the balcony rail hung upside down in the air. Siren wailing, light bar flashing, a police cruiser careened into the parking lot and skidded to a stop by the crash site. The crowd regrouped and multiplied as a sheriff's deputy marched over to the crumpled vehicle. An ambulance and fire truck pulled up as close as they could. Paramedics rushed to the scene, and the area, including Angelica's car, was sealed off with yellow tape. Everything happened fast, leaving her dazed and confused.

Within minutes, a police officer was preparing to interview her while the Epsteins were led away in a different direction. Angelica wanted to reach out her hand to them. *Dear buyers, adieu!*

"Ma'am? Excuse me? Can you tell me what happened?"

Reluctantly, she returned her attention to the cop whose trunk-size arms bulged from short, dark green sleeves, his chest muscles ready to pop the buttons off his shirt.

"I looked up and saw Peter Bedford in the air," she recounted, staring up at the cop's rugged jaw and startling blue eyes. "He wasn't shouting or anything, although he was sort of flapping his arms. Or maybe I'm imagining that."

The officer took notes. "Did you know the victim?" he asked.

"He was my client. I'd just been with him upstairs."

The cop raised an eyebrow. "Your client, you say?"

"I'm a real estate agent."

"Oh. Right." He scribbled in his pad. "Was anyone else with you at the condo?"

"Not when I left. The Epsteins, the elderly couple I was with? They left before me. They just bought his unit."

"Could your buyers have returned to the condo? You know, buyer's remorse? Things might have gotten out of hand."

"You mean they might have pushed Peter Bedford off the balcony? Impossible. You saw how elderly they are. They're adorable!"

The officer cleared his throat, expressing skepticism. "What do you actually know about these people?"

"They're from New York State. They gave me a check to

deposit in escrow."

"How d'you know the check's genuine?"

"Of course it's genuine," Angelica said defensively, even as her mind clouded over in doubt. "Why would they want to murder Peter Bedford? Why would anybody?"

"That's what we need to find out." The cop flipped his pad shut. "I'm going to have to take you down to the station."

"Why?" Angelica cried.

"Ma'am, you're a key witness in the case."

He marched her to his green-on-white cruiser, chest puffed out in self-importance. Angelica clambered into the back, never having set foot inside a police car before today. The interior smelled of sugary donuts, stale cigarettes, and the vaguest suggestion of vomit. Had Macho Cop never heard of Kick-Butt Air Freshener? Funny how the brain focused on trivial details in the midst of a crisis, she reflected. Her mind still refused to believe what had happened.

Just as she was hoping that nobody would recognize her, a man with a camera stepped out of the gawping crowd and snapped a shot of her face. Terrific, she thought: her picture spread all over the front page of the local papers above the story of her dead client. Broker Bob would have a fit. That, however, was the least of her worries, she thought as the patrol car sped her off to the station.

19

*M*acho Cop led her into an interview room, explaining that the two detectives assigned to the case would be along shortly to take her statement. Angelica declined his offer of coffee. She thought with regret how she would have been at lunch with Kathy, digging into Delilah's Delectable Passion Fruit Cheesecake in celebration of her sale, had Bedford not fallen from his balcony. And then she remembered his wife. With a numb sense of unreality, she dialed the Manhattan number on her cell phone.

Bella Bedford's Southern accent slid into her ear, slow and sweet as molasses. "Angelica! Tell me you have good news! You sold the condo!"

"Well," Angelica began, wondering how best to phrase the situation.

"Didn't you have a meeting with a prospect today?"

"Yes, we do have a buyer for the condo. At least, we had one. But, Mrs. Bedford, your husband . . . well, he had an accident."

"Oh? What sort of accident?"

Angelica's throat went dry. The delicate conversation she had often imagined having with her client revolved around her husband's elevated testosterone levels, not his untimely departure from this world. "I can't begin to tell you how sorry I am, Mrs. Bedford," she blurted, "but the fact is, he's—he's dead!" Silence. "Mrs. Bedford, are you still there?"

"What do you mean *dead?*" her client demanded.

"Dead in every sense of the word. He fell from the condo balcony onto his car."

Mrs. Bedford gasped. "The Astie?"

"I'm afraid so." Angelica nodded her thanks to Macho Cop who set a Dixie cup of water on the table in front of her. "I'm at the police station waiting to give a statement."

"You mean you were with him when he fell?"

"I was in the parking lot with the buyers. I don't know what happened." She broke off as two plain-clothes police officers replaced Macho Cop in the interview room. "Mrs. Bedford? The detectives are here. I'll call you later, okay? I'm so, so sorry for your loss," she mumbled, unsure at this point whether she was referring to Peter Bedford or to the exorbitantly expensive car.

"It was his birthday, you know," Bella said in a hoarse whisper. "I was just about to call him."

"Peter Bedford's wife?" one of the detectives inquired when she ended the call.

"Yes. She's in New York."

"How did she take it?"

"Pretty well, I thought." Considering she had lost a husband and a major asset all in one day.

The detectives drew up chairs and introduced themselves. Byron Wright, who had been doing the talking so far, was middle-aged and nondescript, unlike his younger partner, Larry Frye, whose skin had the pale transparency of a vampire, and who wore a narrow, blood-red tie.

"You informed the officer you saw Bedford fall and land on his car, correct?" Detective Wright asked, flicking ash off his rolled up shirt cuff. "Can you tell us what happened at the meeting with your client prior to this incident?"

"Well," Angelica began, "We'd been discussing contract terms with the buyers. Then Dr. Epstein left with his wife, and I chatted with Mr. Bedford for a few minutes."

"And what was the nature of your conversation with your client?"

"We talked about getting the sales agreement back to him to sign. And about how pleased we were to have a cash buyer. Not that it really makes a difference, but it can help move things along."

Wright nodded wearily as though he had been through the mortgage process a thousand times. "And how would you describe his frame of mind at that point?"

Angelica fixed the laminated wood table in concentration. She had agreed to toast the sale with Bedford the following day when she delivered the contract. "He seemed happy," she told Wright.

"Not in the mood for suicide then?" Frye quipped, eyes red-rimmed as though he had been up all night bloodsucking the tender flesh of virgins.

"At first I thought he was flying."

"You mean, like a bird, or what?"

"I thought maybe it was a stunt."

"A man falls from the eighth floor and here you're talking bird and James Bond?" Detective Frye spread his hands wide for an explanation.

"He was a bit of a dare-devil, if you must know!" Angelica cited his revoked commercial pilot's license and the cracker-jack box he had delivered to her office.

Frye yanked loose the knot in his tie. "Seems a lot of trouble to go to, putting something like that together." He folded his arms on the table. "I'm not buying business relationship. Here's this rich airline pilot sending you gifts. And you single. It just don't add up."

"Some gift!" Angelica interjected.

"Are you still saying it was simply a business relationship?" Wright asked with a sympathetic grimace.

Angelica blushed to her ash brown roots. "Of course."

Frye's eyes lased into hers. "Ms. Lane, we found a coupla condoms in the deceased's bill-fold. Seems suspicious a married man with his wife outta town would have these handy."

"He was having an affair."

"With?"

"A blonde. I walked in on them one morning at the condo."

The detectives leaned in attentively.

"Doin' what exactly?" questioned Frye.

Angelica, losing patience, glanced from one detective to the other. "What do you think?"

"What she look like?"

"I didn't see her face," Angelica said, conjuring up in her mind the pouting doll-like features of a centerfold model. "She had her back to me."

The two men exchanged a meaningful look.

Angelica squirmed in her chair as it dawned on her that they did not appear to believe a word she had told them.

20

"**Y**our name is on the front page of the *Guapa Press* and the *Portofino News*," Kathy exclaimed to Angelica on the phone the next day. "Have you seen the papers yet? I don't think I've ever read anything so exciting in the local news before."

"I haven't left my condo," Angelica replied, massaging her throbbing temples. "Hopefully the story will be cold by tomorrow."

"Doubt it. You're a celebrity, hon. The *Press* headline reads, 'Ex-Pilot Crash Lands onto Aston Martin' and the *PF News* asks, 'Suicide, Accident or Foul Play? Realtor Sees Client Fall to his Death.' There's a nice little write-up about you. I didn't know you had a bachelor's in business studies."

"Neither did I," Angelica snapped, at her wits' end. A "nice little write-up" alongside her client's suspicious death she could do without. "Someone must have given them the wrong information. My degree is in art history."

Kathy lowered her voice to a whisper. "It was probably Broker Bob, talking up the office. Anything for free publicity. You're referred to as, and I quote, 'one of Plum Realty's most valued associates.' "

Angelica swore into the phone. How like Broker Bob to exploit the situation now that he could do nothing to avoid it.

"Feeling any better?" the office manager asked.

"It's awful, Kathy. I kept dreaming about it last night."

In one nightmare, Peter Bedford had risen phoenix-like from the ashes and said, "Angelica, you're not such a bad sport after all." It had spooked her.

Kathy dropped her voice. "Broker Bob wants to speak to you first thing Monday."

"Oh, shoot me now. Look, I have to pick up my car from Plovers Key . . ."

"Need a ride?" Kathy asked without missing a beat. "I can pick you up in my lunch hour."

"You sure you don't mind?"

"You can show me the crime scene."

"I think it was probably an accident."

"It better not be," Kathy retorted. "Bob is screaming about liability."

Angelica groaned with despair. So, now it was liability. She couldn't believe it. How could such an enviable listing have turned out so wrong?

She dreaded returning to Plovers Key, but had no choice. After retrieving her car, she went to stock up on groceries and did not venture outside her community again for the rest of the weekend, hoping to avoid further exposure in the local media.

On Monday morning she left the sanctuary of her home and drove to the office to face Broker Bob. Three days had passed since she opened the exploding box in her cubicle, but so much had happened since then that it felt like a week. She had made and lost a sale in the space of one afternoon, witnessed a fatal accident—or worse, and been grilled by a pair of skeptical detectives. In addition, her reputation was on the line.

As she walked by the conference room, she saw Rick at the oval table in full sales mode with a young couple. "Just sign right here," she imagined him saying. "Press hard."

"Is Broker Bob free?" she asked Kathy, craning her neck

to see if Rick was, in fact, writing up a contract. How unfair that would be when her prize listing had been derailed!

"Hon!" the office manager declared when she saw her. "All anyone's talking about at the office is Peter Bedford's death! I've had people calling in to get the latest scoop. Of course, Broker Bob's in a flap and squawking like crazy. Oh, I suppose I'd better tell him you're here. Good luck," she whispered as she pressed his extension.

Squaring her shoulders, Angelica entered his office.

"Sit down, Angelica," the broker said, pushing his spectacles up his beak. "How are you feeling? I thought perhaps we should discuss the Bedford case. Did you have any inkling the balcony rail was loose? What if Mrs. Bedford sues? Or the Epsteins for that matter, for causing emotional distress?" Spittle flecked his thin lips. "Did they sign the contract? Did the Bedfords sign a seller's disclosure form?"

Angelica marked a patient pause as she always did when people asked a bunch of questions before waiting for the first answer. "Mrs. Bedford signed the form," she explained. "There were no defects to report. The Epsteins didn't mention getting an inspection done. I checked everything I could myself, bar swinging from the balcony rails."

"Don't get cute. I'm simply trying to determine the extent of liability. What's happening about the contract?"

"Dr. Epstein called to apologize for not sending it," Angelica admitted, determined not to let Broker Bob see the depth of her disappointment. "He wants to await the outcome of the police investigation."

"People typically don't want stigmatized properties," opined Broker Bob. "Especially in a buyer's market. This is going to be a tough sell, Angelica, always assuming Mrs. Bedford doesn't pull out."

"Her listing agreement is for six months!"

"Extenuating circumstances. When did you last speak with

her?"

"First thing this morning. I assured her the Epsteins were still interested. The condo is being treated as a crime scene so I can't very well show it to anyone else."

Broker Bob pursed his lips. "This is all very unfortunate. Was the man drinking? Or could it have been a heart attack?" he asked hopefully.

"I guess we'll find out from the autopsy report."

Broker Bob sighed and nodded curtly, dismissing Angelica from his office.

A heart attack *would* be the most acceptable cause of death, she reasoned. Heaven forbid that Bedford was found to be on mind-altering drugs or something scandalous that would prolong the publicity. Or that the rail was indeed found to be defective. Surely Mrs. Bedford wouldn't sue? Only an idiot or someone with a death wish would lean all their weight against a balcony rail on the eighth floor of a building. And Bedford hardly seemed the type to kill himself.

Or was he?

21

With the Plovers Key sale postponed, Angelica set out to meet a former client's nephew who was in a hurry to sell before the bank foreclosed on his house. She had no idea what to expect. A better idea formed as she drew nearer her destination. Desirable proximity to the Gulf diminished with every mile she drove east. Flamingo Circle, located east of new U.S. 41, east of old U.S. 41, and east of the railway tracks, applied the real estate axiom of "location, location, location" three times over in reverse. More depressing still, she discovered when she got there, her referral's neighborhood lay wedged between two trailer parks, the street sign defaced with a familiar four-letter expletive.

At first glance, this was a transitional neighborhood. A few retirees who kept their yards clean and tidy and decorated their lawns with pink plastic flamingos, resisted the downhill trend, but it was evidently a losing battle as, one by one, they died off or drifted into nursing homes, and the street succumbed to an invasion of careless renters. Most of the 1960's bungalows on the circle had their carports converted into extra living space or, in one case, a car repair shop. Duct-taped vehicles and old brown vans swarmed many of the front yards. Angelica felt right at home in her graffiti-ridden Camry.

She continued down the street, locating her prospect's address by process of elimination, a pile of rubble standing where the mailbox should have been. A wizened orange tree bearing pock-marked fruit stood in the front, a sinister omen warding her off with gnarled and twisted branches. She felt tempted to turn around, but she needed this listing. Warily, she got out of her car, having first parked on the far side of the road so the *B* word remained hidden.

"'Ey!" called a weasely man emerging from the carport. Blond-streaked hair straggled down his reddened neck, encircled by a large silver cross. "You the *reelater?*" A can of Old Milwaukee in one hand, cigarette butt in the other, he ambled jauntily down the concrete driveway in paint-splattered jeans and a white muscle vest.

"Rusty Scrob?" Angelica asked with little hope of it being anyone else. "I couldn't see a mailbox."

"Yup." Squinting in the direction of the rock pile, the man spewed out a cloud of cheap tobacco. "Work-in-progress," he drawled. "I'm buildin' a post."

A psychedelic plastic mailbox in the shape of a giant fishing lure glimmered beside the rubble, trailing a shiny hook. Scrob sucked on a nicotine-stained tooth as he contemplated his creation. Then, after taking a last drag of the cigarette, he pitched the butt into the neighbor's yard.

Angelica turned away under the pretext of surveying the carport. The bumper sticker on a Caprice sedan propped up on cinder blocks announced, *"Keep honking . . . I'm reloading."* Below it, another slyly proclaimed, *"I'd rather be shootin' than fishin'."*

By the side of the house, the hood of a Chevy pickup yawned, exposing rusted coils and boxes.

"Looks like a hurricane swept through your yard," she observed as she stumbled among the old tires, a flagless flagpole, torn basketball net, kid's bicycle, and pogo stick, all strewn across the patchy Bahia grass.

"The wife brung the kids for the weekend," Scrob was in

the midst of explaining when a snarling black pit bull confronted her at the corner of the house.

"Quit that, ya hear?" Scrob thumped the dog's flank.

Yelping, it cowered in submission at the end of a frayed rope. Its owner proudly waved his beer can toward a plywood structure in whose wire enclosure clucked a motley collection of scraggly fowl.

Angelica stared. "And what's this other thing?" she demanded, pointing to a similar arrangement of plywood and chicken wire.

Scrob scratched the graying sandpaper stubble on his chin. "That's fer ferrets. Ain't got none yet."

"Well, don't." So disconcerted was she by the prospect of showing a house with ferrets that she almost fell into an avocado-hued bathtub camouflaged by the weeds.

Scrob kicked the ex-fixture with his work boot. "This here's gonna be a rainwater fish pond."

Angelica stifled a wail of hysterical laughter as the phrase "starter home" began to take on a whole new definition, wherein everything had been started—and left unfinished. Scrob's bungalow was by far and away the worst on the block. It was an eyesore, a lemon, a blight on the landscape. Perhaps she could use its lamentable condition as a marketing strategy: *Fixer-upper beyond your wildest dreams!* Whatever she did, she would have to be very creative.

There must be some feature she could hang an ad on, she thought stoically as she approached the lanai extension, where electrical icicles sagged from the eves of a black shingle roof.

Scrob followed her gaze. "New ruff."

"You didn't do it yourself, did you?" she asked, stepping back a safe distance.

"Naw." Scrob downed the rest of his beer and lobbed the can into the hedge. "My brother put that on 'fore he runned off with my wife. Thou shalt not covert yer brother's wife, the Lord says. Rufus died for his sins, tha's a fact." His staccato laugh resembled a demented hyena's. "Wanna take a look inside?" he asked.

Angelica did not, and was saved by a call from Detective Wright asking her to come down to the station immediately. She never dreamed she would be glad to hear from the cops, but Rusty Scrob was the scrubbiest individual she had ever had the misfortune to meet, and she could not get away fast enough.

At the same time, she knew she could not afford to be choosy, with the Peyntons dragging their feet and the Plovers Key condo on hold. With any luck, the detective had information that would wrap up the Bedford case so she could begin to put the whole ordeal behind her and get on with her life.

22

"*T*hanks for coming," Wright said, indicating a chair in the interview room.

Angelica sat across the table from the two detectives, as before; only, this time a tape recorder stood between them.

"There've been some interesting developments," Wright explained. Angelica could not help but notice that his shirt had developed a gravy stain on the pocket since she last saw him. "And we're hoping you can help us shed some light on a coupla things," he added.

She drew up her chair. "I hope so."

"Good. We're going to record our conversation because neither of us old cops ever did learn shorthand." Wright shrugged in woefulness at their inadequacy and pressed a button on the machine. A red light came on and twin spools started spinning. He dictated the date, time, location, and persons present, asking Angelica to state her full name.

Angelica suddenly felt uneasy. Her stomach had not flipped over this way since she rode the Montu at Busch Gardens. She reminded herself she was simply helping the police with their inquiries. Isn't that what they said of people of interest? Was she a person of interest in this case?

"First we have photos to show you," Detective Sergeant Frye said, a malevolent gleam in his violet eyes.

She didn't think she would be able to positively identify anyone other than Bedford, but she was willing to give it a try. The detective slid two five by seven-inch shots across the table. Picking up the top one, she stared at it, and then looked closer.

"Is that you?" he asked.

Angelica wanted to disappear through the floor. The machine whirred on, recording dead air. "No. I mean, it's not how it looks," she rasped.

Wright sucked in his breath, nodding sympathetically. "Looks like Bedford and you are getting real cozy there on the sofa."

"Compromising stuff," Frye chimed in, clearly enjoying seeing her squirm.

Angelica peered at the grainy black and white freeze-frame. Despite the blurry quality, there could be no denying whose legs were raised either side of Bedford's hairy, muscular ones, her arms flung akimbo on the cushions. With a shaky hand she picked up the second photo. This one showed her in Bedford's embrace as they stood by the king-size bed the morning he had shown her the bird of prey on the balcony.

"I don't understand," she murmured, her face blazing like a Florida sunset. "Where did these come from?"

"Caught in the act, huh?" Detective Frye mocked.

"I asked him to stop!" Angelica protested. "And he did. Twice!" Tears of shame and frustration sprang to her eyes. "You have to believe me! Who took these pictures, anyway?" she demanded.

Wright produced a wad of grubby tissues from his pocket. "Don't distress yourself, Ms. Lane. We have to ask these questions, you understand."

"Do I have to answer them?"

"It'll look better for you if you do."

Angelica blew her nose. "Can you tell me what you know about Peter Bedford's death?"

The detective flattened his beefy hands on the table. "Okay. How about we work together, see if we can get on the same page? We give you information. You give us information."

Angelica nodded. This sounded reasonable enough.

"We'll go first," the detective said. "First off, there were surveillance cameras in the condo. Like those you find in stores? Only these weren't angled at entry points for security purposes."

"Someone was spying?"

"Right. Actually, a private investigator installed them for Annabella Bedford. One was hidden in a bookshelf in the living room above the sofa. The other, with a wide-angle lens, was concealed behind a Picasso knock-off in the bedroom. The eye of the camera looked through a hole in the painting. Seems Mrs. Bedford wanted proof that her husband was having an affair."

"Not with me!"

Wright flipped his palm. "Hey, believe me, Ms. Lane, you weren't the only girl on film."

"However," Frye said, spinning a third photo across the table. "You were also seen having dinner with your client. Classy French joint. Trez romantique," he added suggestively in an exaggerated French accent.

"We went to dinner, yes," Angelica admitted. "But just the one time."

"What else we gonna find out?" Frye asked. "We got you two with your hands all over each other, and him taking you to a four star restaurant. We even got a picture of you sharing drinks on the condo balcony."

Angelica slumped in her chair and rubbed her forehead. "That's all there is."

Frye shook his head. "No, see now, the gumshoe followed Bedford's car to your home one night. Actually saw him walk up to your front door."

"You've got it all wrong!" Angelica cried. "I'm being framed! You've got to believe me!"

The detectives looked bored, as though they had heard it all before.

"Now, we know he didn't go inside," Wright conceded.

Angelica breathed a sigh of relief.

"But you gotta understand that we know you lied to us," Frye told her. "About having a business relationship. So now we want truthful answers."

She nodded, confused about what she had said. She had tried to be truthful. Why had the private eye been following her? Or had he been following Bedford?

"For instance," Wright added, "we want to know who Bedford might have introduced you to within his circle of friends and acquaintance."

Angelica's gaze gravitated back to the gravy stain on the detective's shirt, which blossomed before her eyes beneath the fluorescent lighting. Closing them, she wracked her brain for any tidbit of information that might help get her out of this mess.

"Peter Bedford mentioned a colleague who might be interested in purchasing a property," she said at last, "but I don't remember his name, and I never met him."

"Anything at all you can give us on this colleague?" Frye asked.

"Not much, except that I assumed he must be rich because he was looking for a place on the beach." She thought for a moment. "Oh! And Bedford said he owned a big pet food company in Florida. Divine Canine Eats & Treats."

The detectives twitched.

"That's good, Ms. Lane," Wright said with a nod of approval. "Anything else?"

"I remember because my dog likes that brand. He's very picky. I can't think of anything else."

"You've been very helpful."

Angelica wet her lips, encouraged to ask a few questions of her own. "So, can you tell me what happened?"

"We can tell you that forensic evidence suggests Bedford was pushed over the balcony."

Angelica gasped. "He was murdered? For real?"

"For real," Frye confirmed with a sardonic smirk.

"I'm not a suspect, am I?" She wondered, belatedly, if she should have asked for a lawyer to be present. She hoped she hadn't incriminated herself. But she was innocent! "How do you know he was murdered?" she asked.

Wright paused before replying, as though weighing how much information he should divulge. "The spot where he landed wasn't consistent with falling. He must've been propelled forward with force in order to land where his car was parked. Plus, an autopsy report showed up bruises around his neck that indicate there was some sort of struggle before he went over the balcony."

Glacial fear slid down her spine. Terrifying enough to remember Peter Bedford plummeting to his death without having to think about someone actually pushing him over the rail. Not the Epsteins, surely. They would not have had time, materializing in the parking lot just moments after Bedford landed on his car.

"Did you see anyone on your way out the building?"

Angelica forced herself to remember. "I took the elevator. I can't recall if I saw anyone in the lobby. There's usually a concierge and one or two other people down there."

"Fine, okay." Detective Wright checked his watch. "One last question. Did Bedford mention what he might be doing later that day?"

"He said he couldn't offer me lunch because he had an

engagement."

"A lunch engagement?" probed Detective Frye.

Angelica considered for a moment. She had picked up on the word "engagement" because she wondered at the time if he was lunching with the blonde. "I think so. But he didn't say who with."

"Thank you, Ms. Lane." Detective Wright spoke into the machine and clicked a button.

"Am I free to go?" Angelica pleaded.

"For now. But we may need to talk to you again." Wright escorted her into the corridor. "And don't discuss this case with anyone. If the killer's out there, we don't want him knowing we're onto him. Got it?"

"It's a him?"

The detective smiled enigmatically. "Call us if you remember anything else. And, Ms. Lane? Be vigilant at all times. The murderer might be watching you."

Angelica left the station house in a daze. As she stepped off the curb, a black SUV swerved in her path, missing her by mere inches. The driver honked, but the dark tint on the windows prevented her from seeing inside the vehicle. She stared after it, shaken by her close shave. It wasn't easy to be vigilant and clear-headed when she had just been informed there was a killer on the loose.

23

*M*urder? Who could have murdered Peter Bedford? Angelica pondered the possibilities as she drove to the office. Surely not his own wife? But Bella had set up the video cameras on him because she thought he was having an affair. She had motive. She may have hoped to cash in on a life insurance policy. She may have hired a hit man.

Did Bella know about *her?* Had she seen the tapes? Impossible. She would have canceled the listing with Plum Realty. Angelica braked violently at an amber light. Think, think. Who else? Suddenly, a jolt from behind catapulted her car from its stationary position with a resounding thud and crumpling of metal, slamming her into her seat belt. Looking over her shoulder, she saw that a BMW had rear-ended her.

A female lawyer from New York turned out to be the driver. Angelica wrung her hands at the dent in her bumper. How much more abuse was she supposed to take? She began to feel seriously paranoid.

"You always brake at the last second?" the lawyer cross-examined her in a Brooklyn accent. "What was I supposed to do? Fly over you?"

"You're supposed to anticipate," Angelica replied.

"Really? Anticipate. I see. Very interesting." The attorney walked around in a tight circle, brandishing her finger. She wore what looked to be white support hose under her suit, though she didn't look much older than Angelica, and the weather was warm. "Well, excuse me for not anticipating better. How much anticipating are people behind you expected to do?"

"If you hadn't been *tawking* on your cell phone, you might not have run into me," Angelica snapped. "The light was orange."

"I was not on my phone," the lawyer denied categorically.

"I saw you."

"Well, that's rich!—"

"Ladies, ladies," the traffic cop intervened. "It's only a fender bender. As long as no one got hurt."

"I may have mild whiplash," Angelica said as the cop handed the lawyer a ticket.

"Failure to anticipate," Angelica explained smugly.

"I'll contest this in court!"

"That's your privilege, ma'am," the cop said, ambling back to his vehicle.

"Did you see what someone scratched on her car?" Lawyer Lady called after him. "B-I-T-C-H! Can't say I'm surprised . . ."

Angelica drove on to the office where Rick Powers met her with a groping hug on her way to her cubicle. "Angelica, you poor thing! What you must be going through! The *Press* is saying Bedford was pushed off the balcony. And to think you were with him just moments before!"

Was there no respite? She thought she felt a stiffness in her neck. "The media is grasping at straws," she told Rick. "There is probably a perfectly innocent explanation for his death."

The detectives had suggested he was murdered, based on where he landed, but, knowing Bedford, he might have been trying to imitate the kestrel and taken a flying leap into the air, dragging the balcony rail with him.

Not highly probable, she allowed.

"Ms. Lane!" Broker Bob's voice brayed across the sales area, interrupting her thoughts. "A moment of your time, please."

"Excuse me," Angelica said, squeezing past Rick's immaculately attired form.

Broker Bob had summoned her by her last name. This did not bode well. She entered his office and closed the door behind her.

Broker Bob clasped his hands on top of his desk. "Sit down, Ms. Lane. Some unpleasantness, I'm afraid." He proceeded to clear his throat. "I received a complaint from your Flamingo Circle client, Russell Scrob."

"He's just a suspect at this point," Angelica said. "I mean, a prospect."

Sighing, Broker Bob shook his head. "The Bedford case is clearly affecting you. Perhaps you should consider taking some time off. What have you got on your plate?"

"Plovers Key is in limbo right now, as you know," she said, trying to keep the panic from her voice. "Palm Meadow is my only other listing. Other than Flamingo Circle, I guess."

"I'm sorry, Angelica. You can kiss Flamingo goodbye. Mr. Scrob said . . ." Here Broker Bob scratched his beaky nose. "Well, to paraphrase, he said you were a, uh, stuck-up bitch."

Angelica's jaw fell open. That word again, first scratched on her car, and now out of that yahoo's mouth.

"I sent Jenn to try and smooth things over," Broker Bob explained. "You'll still get a referral fee as the procuring agent, but I strongly suggest you don't go back there."

"I'm crushed," Angelica told him.

Broker Bob laced his fingers and wiggled his thumbs. "No call for sarcasm, Angelica. A listing is a listing, and referrals are a Realtor's lifeline. When I started out in this business, I spent evenings distributing flyers on car windshields all over town. No listing was too small or too far."

He swept a hand toward the framed awards and certificates on his walls. "Jenn is not above a buck and a quarter sale," he said to grind in his point.

"Scrob's property won't fetch one hundred and twenty-five thousand dollars!" Angelica expostulated. Not even close. What was Broker Bob smoking? "It's falling apart. There's junk in the yard and zero curb appeal."

"You could have offered to pay him fifty bucks just to get rid of it and donate to Goodwill. Curb appeal! Yellow's the color. Yellow flowers. Yellow pots! Invest a little and make a lot!"

"There's no way you could give Rusty Scrob any curb appeal."

"Let's not get snippy." Broker Bob pulled off his spectacles and pinched the bridge of his nose, letting the gold frame dangle from his fingers. "Just see if you can hold on to Palm Meadow without having the client walk or die on you, okay?" He waggled his fingers to indicate she could leave.

Angelica slid from her chair and turned toward the door, rolling her eyes. Broker Bob had to be the biggest lunatic in real estate. Outside his office, she found Jenn chatting to Kathy.

"So. You met Rusty the Redneck?" Angelica said to the young agent.

"Oh-my-God!" Jenn exclaimed. "I was just telling Kathy he keeps an eight-foot python under the bed!"

Angelica raised an eyebrow, impressed by Jenn's spunk. "You went inside?"

Jenn nodded. "Didn't really want to. The whole place doesn't show at all well."

"Tell me about it. It's like Old McDonald's Farm, isn't it? Only more exotic. Has he got any ferrets yet?"

"Ferrets? Yikes! No, I didn't see any of those, just an empty cage. The other has skinny chickens in it."

Angelica recalled the forlorn, clucking fowl. "Did Mr. Scrob brag to you about his Do-It-Yourself achievements?"

"D.U.I., you mean," Jenn exclaimed. "I never saw so many beer cans in a driveway. Or cigarette butts." She paused, looking down at her pointy shoes. "All the same, I do feel bad about Broker Bob taking the listing away from you."

Angelica shrugged. "It's okay. This way I still get something. And I really didn't have the heart for it after everything that's happened."

"I know. You get a plum listing like Plovers Key and then *ka-boom!* Next stop, Casa Scrob."

"That pretty much sums it up," Angelica agreed. "If one more thing goes wrong, I think I'll take Broker Bob's advice and go on vacation." She paused. "On second thoughts, that's just what he wants me to do, and I wouldn't give him the satisfaction."

"Careful," Kathy warned her. "Broker Bob is itching to get rid of you so he can disassociate the firm from the murder at Plovers Key. Don't give him any excuses."

"Was it really a murder?" Jenn asked. "Have they ruled out natural causes?"

"He was a fit fifty-three-year-old," Angelica said, wishing bad health had been the cause of death, after all. There had certainly not been anything wrong with his libido.

"In any case, it's just as well he landed on his car," Jenn said. "Can you imagine the mess in the parking lot if he'd hit the ground?"

"Thanks for the gory visual," Kathy remarked, heading back toward the front desk.

Angelica shuddered.

24

*T*he walls of her condo closed in around her. Angelica's head felt like it might explode. She could not stop thinking about the interview at the police station and the most recent damage to her car, thanks to the yakking attorney from Brooklyn. Add to that, Broker Bob's veiled threat. Most brokers didn't like their agents taking vacation time. The implication didn't bode well in the least.

In need of fresh air, she took Hercules to the deserted pool, where she left him to wander within the confines of the white aluminum fence while she performed laps and mulled over what she knew about the Bedford case. Wright had given nothing away regarding the alleged perpetrator's identity or even if the police knew who it was. Granted, the detective had said "he," but Wright could have been purposely trying to mislead her, although he and his partner had seemed interested in Bedford's colleague. It was all extremely perplexing.

As she watched Hercules ferret under a pool recliner, an unwelcome vision of Rusty Scrob interrupted her train of thought. Her pet trotted toward her and lay with his paws hanging over the lip of the pool. She playfully flicked water at him, recalling the vicious creature that Scrob kept tied to the end of a rope. Probably not the dog's fault it was mean. Watching Scrob at work on his home improvement projects would send anyone over the edge.

She swam to the shallow end and splashed up the steps. As she stooped to sweep her towel off a poolside chair, Hercules charged past her, his sharp bark ricocheting off the concrete slab. Staring after him, she spotted a movement in the red hibiscus bushes on the other side of the fence.

"Hey!" she yelled, glimpsing a darkly clad figure retreating behind a waterfall.

Wrapping her towel tightly around her, she wondered if she should call the police. Or was she just being paranoid, as Peter Bedford had so glibly accused her? If so, she became increasingly suspicious over the next few days when a black Ford Explorer tailed her car to the dry cleaner's, the bank, the grocery store, and the realty office. She wondered if it was the same SUV that had almost run her over at the police station.

She dismissed the idea of calling the cops, fearing the two detectives might somehow turn this new development around on her, as they had done before. Rather than draw more attention to herself, she decided to enlist Kathy's help, having thought up a plan to outsmart the stalker. She did not pause long enough to consider the danger of such a maneuver. She just knew she had to do something.

At first the office manager refused on the grounds the plan was too risky, only coming around when Angelica pleaded and bribed her with lunch at Delilah's.

"Well, okay. I could use a bit of excitement in my life," Kathy finally agreed.

The next afternoon, they waited at the office until everyone had left, and then they swapped clothes. Kathy, who liked to experiment with her hair, had brought from home a brown bobbed wig along with a curly red one. Handing Angelica the office keys, she left first, coiffed as the brunette. Angelica watched through the window as her friend got into the white Camry. After making a few final adjustments to her own disguise, she locked the front door and followed in Kathy's silver VW Jetta.

Turning onto the highway, she headed south on U.S. 41, careful to leave several car lengths between the vehicles and from time to time changing lanes so the driver of the SUV would not see through the ruse. So far, however, no sign of a tail. Shopping plazas streamed by in dreary procession, interrupted by traffic lights, the corner of each intersection anchored by a bank or a chain pharmacy, or yet another furniture store.

Suddenly, as Angelica looked up from searching for the switch to the headlights of Kathy's car, the black SUV loomed into her rearview mirror, dodging and weaving in the rush hour traffic. There was no mistaking the illegally tinted windows and the distinctive brush guard around the fender. The moment it passed her, she called Kathy on her cell and prepared to give chase. Unfortunately, early-birds returning home with their hoards of leftover bread rolls and stolen Sweet n' Low hogged the passing lane, and Angelica lost sight of her pursuer. She beat the heel of her palm on the wheel.

"It's on my tail," Kathy reported seconds later. "It took the bait. But I don't like the look of it. How d'you know this isn't the same person who bumped off Bedford?"

"If Bedford *was* bumped off. We don't know that for sure. Detectives play games, and I don't trust Frye. In fact, I'm convinced he's Dracula incarnate."

"You've been watching too many vampire movies."

"The stalker has had plenty of opportunity to get rid of me if he or she wanted. But, if you're worried, we can try and shake him."

"Just stay close," Kathy replied.

The cars ahead picked up speed, enabling Angelica to zip in behind the black vehicle, sandwiching it between the Jetta and the Camry. "License number D-E-X six-niner-zero," she dictated into the phone.

"You are so busted, Buster," Kathy crowed. "My friend at the DMV will run the number on Monday. Let's continue to the mall, just to be sure we got the right person."

She turned into the main entrance, the SUV shadowing her as Angelica pursued it in turn.

"Circle around while I park," she told Kathy. "I'll be waiting inside Macy's to see if anyone follows you inside. Okay, I found a space. Get ready."

"Ten-four," Kathy confirmed.

Angelica ran across the parking lot, phone glued to her ear.

"I'm getting out of the car now," Kathy informed her. "I hope our stalker doesn't notice you put on fifteen pounds! Jeez, these heels are killing me."

Angelica positioned herself behind a shoe rack facing the entrance, only to be startled minutes later when her likeness in the form of a bewigged Kathy walked through the glass doors.

"I'm right behind you," she told Kathy before breaking phone contact.

She tailed her friend through the busy perfume department and past carousels of clothes to the mall exit. They entered an interior maze of boutiques. She felt self-conscious in her red wig and faux leopard skin raincoat, although a biker in a black leather jacket actually whistled at her as she followed Kathy into a novelty store.

Kathy pulled her behind a stand of red and green joke gifts and gizmos. "Did you see anyone who might be D-E-X six-nine-zero?" she whispered urgently.

"No, it's too busy. You did great, Kathy. That's a fantastic disguise. Even I thought it was me when you walked through the door. "

They pulled off their wigs and exchanged coats. Kathy opened her compact and began stacking her cropped gray hair back into place between her fingers. "What a hoot. We'll find out who the SUV is registered to, and you can decide if you want to involve the police. There's also the incident at the pool, remember."

"I hadn't forgotten."

They paused outside the store and watched the shoppers milling around the holiday displays, but no one stood out as truly suspicious among the mob of teenage mall rats and harassed women with hyper kids in tow.

"Plus, you've got to factor in the graffiti on your car," Kathy continued. "It's all adding up, and it doesn't look good."

Angelica had added it up—and almost lost count.

25

*T*he next morning, sipping coffee on her lanai in her pajamas, Angelica scanned the leisure section of the local newspaper, having first perused the front pages for stories relating to the Plovers Key mystery, and found nothing new. She had started to sketch the lake and fountain that formed the focal point of the landscaping amid the cluster of low-rise condominium blocks out back, with the intention of developing it into a watercolor for her mother's new house. Only, her heart was not in it and, in any case, she doubted Susan would ever display the picture, except perhaps when Angelica visited, if even then.

Spotting an advertisement for an outdoor art fair in town, she resolved to go and make a start on her Christmas shopping, to take her mind off things. At the very least, it would help fill in time until Monday, when she would receive an answer from the Department of Motor Vehicles about who had tailed Kathy to the mall in the black SUV. As she took her empty mug to the kitchen, the phone rang.

"Claire!"

"Hi, Jelly. Sorry I didn't get back to you sooner. I was busy with work and—"

"You okay?"

"Great. Why?"

"Your letter! What was all that about?"

"Oh, that can wait until Christmas. I'd rather tell you in

person."

Angelica grit her teeth. "You could give me a hint. I've been so worried."

"I'll tell you when I see you in Oregon, Jelly."

It became clear that Claire, maddening as she was, could not be prevailed upon to divulge her secret. At least her sister wasn't sick or in danger, as she had feared.

"I thought about painting a landscape for Mom's house," she said, changing subject. "Do you think she'd like it?"

"Probably not. And that's not a reflection on your talent, Jelly. But you know how she feels about 'homemade' gifts."

"I keep hoping she'll change."

The projects her two daughters had made at school had never found shelf or wall space in the family home. In fact, Susan had never encouraged her eldest to pursue painting, deeming it a bohemian and unstable endeavor. Claire, the artier of the two sisters, had parlayed her creativity into a career in cosmetology, specializing in hair color and make-up application.

"But everybody at the salon loves your balloon picture," Claire enthused. "I keep hoping you'll be discovered by someone famous and become the next Peter Max, or whatever."

"I don't have such aspirations. I just thought it would be nice to give her something personal."

"Give it to me instead. Please? Sam says we need to make our apartment look less like a waiting room."

Angelica laughed because this was so true of her sister, whose living quarters always had a transitory feel about them, perhaps a product of their being raised as army brats and moving from place to place. Claire had given up on decorating the succession of bedrooms. For Angelica, however, a sense of permanence had become essential, which was why the purchase of her first home had meant so much to her.

"What's going on with you?" Claire prodded.

Angelica wondered where to begin. A lot had been going on. She attempted to fill her sister in on the Bedford case and related the perplexing sequence of events surrounding it. She played everything down, knowing Claire would repeat the news to their parents. Her mother would worry, as would her dad, and they both lived too far away to do anything, even if something could be done.

After the call, Angelica showered and dressed. Tucking Hercules under her arm, she made for the detached garage, wincing anew when she saw the offending letters scraped on the passenger side of her car. She unearthed a roll of duct tape, cut off a length with a pair of garden shears, and applied it to the door panel. Together with the damaged bumper, the car resembled a clunker from Scrob's neighborhood—but at least the word was concealed.

Senses on high alert for the black SUV, she headed into the center of town. The art fair occupied the lot of a large chain store. Managing to grab a convenient parking space as someone was leaving, she was soon meandering through the white-tented booths, while Hercules trotted close on her heels. All of a sudden, an oil painting, one among a collection of still lifes, caught her eye.

She could almost smell the purple vine flowering over the sun-drenched balustrade, all but touch the peeling green paint on the solitary wooden chair in the shade. The picture was so realistic, in fact, that she half expected someone to step onto the canvas at any moment and retrieve the straw hat trailing a white ribbon perched on the chair's finial. The scene evoked a memory, an emotion, a yearning for something lost.

"Two hundred and fifty dollars," said the woman seated behind a folding table in answer to her inquiry. "It's called

'Solitude.' I painted it on a trip to Naples in Italy last year."

Angelica stood back to view the picture from a distance. It would look fabulous in her living room. But two hundred and fifty dollars! If she had sold the Plovers Key condo, she'd be shopping at Saks and browsing in upscale galleries. As it was, she had to watch every dime. The leash jerked in her hand. Pulled in the dog's direction, she spotted a large man in sunglasses dodge out of sight.

Gathering up Hercules, she jogged after the blond ponytail, breaking into a run as the stranger was about to turn at the end of a row of booths. She yelled after him. He halted in his tracks and pivoted around to face her, hands thrust into the pockets of his black jeans.

"You're the biker from the mall!" she exclaimed in self-righteous indignation while Hercules craned his neck at him from her arms.

"Look," the man said, glancing around at the passers-by as though inviting them to bear witness to the crazy woman and her dog. "I don't want to seem rude, but do I know you?"

"You made a pass at me yesterday evening."

He regarded her dubiously.

"I was wearing—oh!" she exclaimed, remembering what she had on: a red wig and a faux leopard skin coat. "You have unbelievably bad taste in women," she blurted, visualizing the horrible disguise.

"If you say so."

He sauntered away, throwing a wave over his shoulder, leaving Angelica in some doubt as to whether he was, in fact, the guy from the mall. She was under considerable stress and could be mistaken. Quite normal under the circumstances. She decided to treat herself to the painting. She needed cheering up. Material deprivation adversely affected the soul, as her mother, a voracious consumer, had often informed her.

Retracing her steps, she stopped to browse in a booth of glass ornaments, where she could not resist buying a jade green perfume bottle trimmed in Indian silver for Claire. She made another stop for fresh-squeezed lemonade at a stand. By the time she returned to the art tent, she found the tripod empty. The canvas she had set her heart on was gone.

The artist opened her hands in mute apology. Sick with disappointment, Angelica left the woman chatting with her customer, and arrived at her car just as the longhaired stranger roared past on a peacock blue Harley bristling with chrome. Hercules growled after him. If that rude biker hadn't caught her attention, she would never have wandered away and lost the picture to someone else. She could not believe her run of bad luck.

She had lost interest in the fair. She might as well go home and clean her condo, and hope Monday brought better news.

26

*T*he next morning Kathy, looking pleased with herself, handed Angelica a piece of paper with a name and address on it.

"Super sleuths that we are," she said with a wink.

"Thank your friend at the DMV for me. I'll head up to Guapa Springs right now." Angelica scrutinized the name again. "Duane Dexter," she murmured.

"Someone could have stolen the SUV," Kathy pointed out in her sensible way. "I still think you should talk to the police. You don't know what you're getting yourself into."

"I want to take a look around first."

"You mean trespass?"

"Don't forget they've been following and harassing *me*."

"If it *is* the same person who keyed your car and made the prank call," Kathy said.

"If I run into trouble, I'll call Detective Wright."

"You could have asked Jenn to go with you, but she didn't show up for floor duty. I hope she's not sick." Kathy gave Angelica a canister of pepper spray from her bag. "Here, take this, hon, just in case."

"You carry this stuff around with you?"

"I do now."

"Sorry I dragged you into this."

"It works on bears and humans, blinding them just long enough to make a getaway," Kathy informed her.

"I won't have to use it on a bear unless it escaped from the zoo." The only bears indigenous to Florida were the small black variety.

Angelica thanked Kathy for the spray and, assuring her she would be fine, headed for her car. Perhaps if she went to the detectives with a solid piece of information gleaned from her investigation, they would clue her in on what else they knew about Bedford's murder. This way, at least, she was doing something, which was better than being a victim—or worse, a suspect. Of course, if Bedford's killer was after her, she could be doing him or her a huge favor by personally delivering herself to their door.

However, Kathy knew where she was going, and it wasn't as if she planned on doing anything dangerous. She was just going to check out the lay of the land. Bolstered by these arguments, she found herself half an hour later in Guapa Springs on a secluded stretch of the Imperial River at the end of an unpaved road abutting a wood. A raccoon slunk into the undergrowth, the only sign of life as, parked at a discreet distance, she surveyed her target, a tin-roof cottage tucked away among dangling Spanish moss and luscious sea grape. Blue and white periwinkles sprouted from the window boxes. Not exactly what she had expected.

Purse over her shoulder, she crunched up the gravel driveway, mounted the steps, and rang the bell. When nobody answered the second ring, she started back down the stairs. At least she had tried. Just then, the front door flew open, and she jumped. The biker she had spoken to at the art fair stood on the porch drying his hands on a dishcloth, showing no sign of recognition. Her nerve collapsed.

"Hi," she said with a fake smile.

He scrutinized her face impassively. "You an Avon lady? Hon—ey!" he yelled over his shoulder.

What was she going to do now? She had nothing to sell

except for a stub of lipstick and a wand of dried-out mascara. Perhaps she should just spray the chemical at him and make a run for it.

"I guess my wife's not home," he said, folding muscular arms across his black T-shirt, exposing an intricate silver tattoo of a Celtic cross on his left bicep. "What do you really want? You're no Avon lady and I'm not married. So let's start over."

"What I want to know is why you've been following me. And don't deny it!"

"Who's following who?" he asked, an amused gleam in his obsidian gray eyes.

She had never seen eyes that color. She took a deep breath. "Duane Dexter?"

"I go by Dex."

"You *are* the owner of a black SUV?"

"Why d'you want to know? You wanna come in?"

In spite of his height, breadth and girth, Duane Dexter seemed to pose no threat to her person, and she was determined, now that she had come this far, to get answers.

"Thank you. It is hot for November. But, in case you get any funny ideas, my office knows exactly where I am. And I'm armed."

Dex raised his hands in mock surrender. "Don't worry, I'm a man of the law. I was making lunch," he added, standing aside as she stepped through the door. She followed him across a hardwood floor encumbered with a black leather sofa and a big screen TV, and entered a galley kitchen, where a crank-operated jalousie window looked out to the brackish river glinting in the sunlight. Picking up a knife, he deftly sliced two enormous tomatoes on a wooden chopping board.

Angelica took in the chipped tile countertops and old-fashioned cuckoo clock on the wall. "Quaint," she said in real estate agent parlance for outmoded and quirky.

"Sandwich?" he asked.

The kitchen looked sanitary enough and her stomach was growling. "Please," she said. "Those tomatoes look really juicy."

"Homegrown. Mayo?"

"Yes, please. The reason I'm here . . ."

"I like rock salt on mine. How about you?"

"That would be good. Anyway . . ."

"Beer?" He ripped off the bottle top against the edge of the counter, which Angelica noticed was scarred from such abuse.

Since he offered no glass, she swigged the beer straight from the bottle, letting it foam refreshingly in her mouth while he plunked a tower of sandwiches onto a plate.

"Come on through," he said, leading her to a screened-in porch overlooking the back of the property.

"I don't believe it!" she cried, pulling up short in front of a painting of a solitary green chair on a terrace. "Did you get that at the art fair? I was going to buy that picture."

"Yeah? I couldn't bring it home on the bike, so I had to go back for it."

"How did you get it framed so fast?"

"Did it myself." Sinking into a wicker rocking chair, he gestured for her to take its twin.

"Would you consider re-selling it to me?" she asked. "I'd pay extra for the frame, of course."

"Why would I do that?"

"Please."

"You are one pushy young lady, huh? Why d'you want it so much?"

"It just, I don't know, tugs at something inside of me. We visited Italy on a family vacation before my parents divorced." Feeling the color mount to her cheeks, Angelica gazed away through the lanai screen to a spreading crepe myrtle tree blooming in dusky pink clusters in the back yard.

He considered for a moment before shaking his head. "Sorry. Finders keepers, losers weepers. You should've bought it while you had the chance."

"I know, but you distracted me. I thought you were spying on me. I really wanted that painting."

"And do you usually get what you want?"

Angelica pondered the question. "Not lately. Quite the reverse, actually. I'm sorry I asked. I wouldn't under normal circumstances."

"These are not normal circumstances?"

Angelica laughed uncomfortably, taken aback by his questions. "Why do I feel like I'm talking to my therapist?"

"You have a therapist?"

"No, I do not! I'm just saying I feel like I should be reclining on a couch, the way you seem to be analyzing me."

"I am not analyzing you," Dex said. "Although you mentioning laying on a couch suggests some interesting subconscious longings."

"I do not have any subconscious longings in that department!"

"But if they were subconscious you wouldn't know about them."

Angelica opened her mouth to deliver a barb, to the effect that he hardly represented her fantasy of the male species, but thought better of it. She was, after all, a guest in his house, and he had made lunch. "Thanks," she said, taking a sandwich from the plate. She hadn't realized how hungry she was and polished off another round.

"You have quite an appetite for such a skinny girl," he remarked. "Any tips? I could stand to lose a few pounds."

"What I have is questions. In fact, I have so many I really don't know where to begin."

"Just fire away."

She brushed crumbs off her cream silk blouse. "Well, first of all, how come you've been following me? Are you a private detective?"

He stretched in his chair and folded his arms. "Darn. You just went and blew my cover." He could not have looked more unconcerned about it.

"I thought private eyes lived in squalid walk-ups with a half dozen deadbolts on the door."

"Sorry to wreck the illusion. We're not in New York."

She sat forward. "Is the biker thing a disguise?"

"What biker thing?"

She let out an exasperated sigh. "The long hair, tattoo, ratty black jeans, leather jacket."

"Don't forget the bike."

"Okay, so you're a private detective. But it *is* Monday, after all, and you're at home."

"I worked Saturday."

"You were at the art fair on Saturday," she corrected him.

"I was being paid to be there."

"Ah-ha! So you *were* following me."

"Purely professionally, I assure you."

Angelica relaxed in her chair. Now she was getting somewhere. "Well, obviously you're not very good at it. But I hope you enjoy tagging me around."

"Not really. It's incredibly boring."

"Oh? And why is that?"

"Because your life, Angelica, is incredibly boring."

"You know my name!"

"I know everything about you. What movies you rent, who your dry cleaner is, your favorite brand of ice cream and feminine hygiene products."

She started to protest, tempted to storm out of the cottage, except that she had come for answers and was determined to get them. "And Peter Bedford's wife put you up to this?" she demanded.

"She hired my company to install surveillance equipment in her condo and follow up on any women her husband might be romancing."

A blush crept over Angelica's face. "You saw the tapes?"

"I'm the one gave them to the police when I heard what happened to Bedford."

Dex's involvement in the investigation opened up such a Pandora's Box of questions that she now felt hard pressed to grasp at a single one. "In that case, why were you still following me?"

"Man, you're really stuck in the groove on that one."

She clenched her fists in her lap. "Look, I don't like being followed and I want to understand why!"

"Okay. I thought you'd make a better case for adultery than his other lay." He held up his palm to prevent her from interrupting. "Don't sweat it. I realize now that you were not having an affair with Bedford. But when he went over the balcony, I decided to pursue a lead of my own. That's why I stayed on your tail. And that's all I'm telling you."

"No more following."

He smiled—a wide, sexy smile. "I'll try not to," he said, "but it'll leave a big void in my life." Rising from his chair, he cleared the plates off the table and strode toward the kitchen.

"Wait!" Angelica called after him.

"Wanna come to Dragonfly Island?" he said, poking his head around the door.

"Where's that?" she asked, not that she had any intention of going there with him.

"In the bay. I'll see if I can find you something to wear. You won't be able to straddle the WaveRunner in that skirt."

Beyond the crepe myrtle, she saw that the yard had been mowed all the way to the river. Tied to a dock, a scooter on a wide ski bobbed on the water. Were those things safe? She had only ever perceived them as a noisy nuisance before. And what about Duane Dexter? Could a private detective be trusted?

She called Kathy on her cell. "Duane Dexter is the P.I. hired by Bella Bedford," she informed the office manager in a hushed voice. "At least, that's what he told me."

"Well, that's a relief. I've been sitting here imagining all sorts of things, like your body being dug up in some remote location."

"You mean, like a deserted island?"

"Hon, is everything okay?"

"I have to go," Angelica said, hearing steps in the kitchen. "I'll call you later."

"This is all I could find," Dex announced from the doorway, holding up a pair of black felty boxer briefs. "They shrank in the wash."

"Are all your clothes black?" Angelica asked, wondering about the dark fabric she had spotted at the swimming pool.

"Why?"

"Just thought you might be into Goth."

He held out his hands in supplication. "There you go again. Pigeonholing."

"Well, first impressions do count for something, you know. Especially in real estate."

"Black is slimming," he explained.

"Were you spying at me at my pool?"

"Maybe. I can check my log."

Angelica pulled the briefs from his hand and examined them. "You've got to be kidding."

"Nobody's going to see," he assured her. "The island is totally private. You can skinny-dip if you want to."

"No way!" she said.

"Suit yourself. Just be sure to bolt the back door when

you leave. The front door is self-locking." He plucked the briefs from her and exited the lanai. "I could've told you who keyed your car," he taunted over his shoulder.

"Okay, I'll come!"

He dropped the briefs on the grass. Angelica scooted across the yard to retrieve them, realizing she had no choice but to put up with Duane Dexter if she hoped to make any sense of what had been happening in her life. Perhaps Dragonfly Island would provide the key.

27

Angelica raced into the kitchen, threw off her shoes and skirt, and pulled on the briefs. She tossed her silk blouse on the chair. No sense in ruining a perfectly good blouse. The camisole top she was wearing underneath would have to do. As an afterthought, she placed one of her business cards on the counter. A thrill of anticipation coursed through her: Now she would discover who had keyed her car.

Hearing the water craft rev up, she hurried into the back yard. She never suspected her afternoon would involve a jaunt on the river with the sort of man her mother had made it her life's mission to steer her daughters away from. Astride the vehicle, Dex navigated it in a figure eight and drew alongside the weathered dock.

"Here, put on this vest and hop on," he instructed, handing her an orange life jacket from off the dock's plank floor.

Grabbing his shoulder, she stepped onto the runner board and swung her leg across the padded seat. The water craft drifted from the sea wall and began chugging downstream past pool enclosures and expanses of back yard, many with boats hoisted on davits. The WaveRunner continued on between sleepy banks shaded by oak trees, cypress and tall sycamore. A branch pointed its finger over the water, spooling a rope swing. From a dried mud ledge, a long-necked ibis dipped its red bill into the murky ripples in search of fish. Focusing on the scenery and the soothing sensation of buoyancy, Angelica felt the tension of recent weeks slip away in the warm breeze.

In a mangrove bay, Dex slowed to idle-speed and pointed to a gray bottle-nosed dolphin and her calf looping through the shallows ten feet away, disappearing only to resurface a moment later, iridescent water skimming off their dorsal fins. Angelica exclaimed in wonder, captivated by the scene of nature playing out before her.

As the Yamaha reached a wide estuary posted with red and green markers, Dex thumbed down on the gas. His ponytail went flying, tickling her chin. A speedboat crossed their path, leaving a choppy wake, and they bumped over the waves, at times airborne before plopping back down into a water trough. Slipping and sliding on the wet seat, Angelica clamped her arms around Dex's waist, fearful of falling off and making a fool of herself.

Finally, beyond the mangroves, she glimpsed the Gulf, blue and serene. Dragonfly Island, which sounded so pleasantly immobile and dry, must be close by. Dex ran the water craft onto a beach. Hundreds of bone white sand dollars slated the shoreline. She dismounted while he pulled the lanyard from his wrist. He removed two towels from under the seat and spread them on a belt of sand between two bundles of bleached driftwood. An empty Osprey nest perched at the top of a tall, leafless trunk. From what she could see, the island appeared to be deserted, except for droves of transparent-winged dragon flies hovering over the mangroves.

Stretched out on a towel, she closed her eyes, inviting the sun to caress her. She could still feel the tingle of wind in her cheeks and taste the salt on her lips. The sun began to press on her eyelids, making her drowsy. Sometime later, she turned her head and saw that Dex wasn't beside her. A short distance down the beach, his clothes dangled from a bush. Puzzled, she sat up on her elbows and caught sight of a pair of bare buttocks before they disappeared into the sea. Hands trailing the surface, he waded to his waist and plunged headlong, proceeding to execute a powerful crawl.

"Show-off", she muttered, settling back on her towel and assessing the situation.

Here she was on a desert island with a nude stranger who had seen the photos of her with Bedford. In fact, Dex was responsible for them. He had handed the tapes over to the police, involving her further in the investigation and leading the detectives to believe she and Bedford were lovers. However, Dex knew more about what was going on than she did, and she was pretty much stuck with him if she wished to pursue her inquiries. She tried not to look as he came walking up the beach, as naked as Adam without the fig leaf, his long hair loosened into dripping ringlets about his shoulders.

"Do you often go around exposing yourself—Fabio?" she called as he grabbed his shorts and stepped into them with his back turned to her. At least he had the decency to do that.

He dropped onto his towel and rolled on his side to face her. "It was either that or wear wet clothes. I thought I had left my trunks in the WaveRunner. Shocked?" he asked.

"No." She would not give him the satisfaction.

He settled on his back with an ironic snort. A *V* formation of pelicans flew overhead in the pellucid blue sky. Only the cry of a seagull and the drone of a biplane interrupted the peace. After a while his breaths became even and deep.

"You were going to tell me who trashed my car," she reminded him.

"Oh, yeah, your car," he said, rousing himself. "Lindy

Weiss. Blonde Californian babe."

"I thought you liked redheads."

"Nah."

"But at the mall you whistled at me."

"I did that for laughs. I knew it was you."

"I see," she said, not sure whether to believe him. "So, this Lindy Weiss, was that Peter Bedford's girlfriend?"

"The same."

"Why did she key my car? And, *hello*, how could you like someone who would do such a thing?"

"Who said I liked her? And what do you care?"

"I don't. I'm just saying this is not a nice person."

"Look, she's sorry. She told me she'd reimburse you for the damage. You just need to get a quote from a body shop."

Angelica flipped onto her side. "She'll really pay up? How did you know it was her?"

"I caught her red-handed in the parking lot. She saw me take her picture and tried to grab the camera. When that didn't work, she got all hysterical, saying how you'd stolen Peter and she wanted to get even."

"Did she set me up on that Palmetto appointment?"

Dex shrugged. "I don't know anything about that."

Perhaps the blonde had pushed Bedford over the balcony in a fit of jealousy. Other than Gloria, Angelica had not found herself the object of envy since elementary school, when Claire had collected her sister's gold stars and flushed them down the commode, leaving one lone star to resurface as evidence of her treachery.

"Now, if only the police would close the case, perhaps I could get on with selling the Plovers Key condo," she told Dex. "By the way, Mrs. Bedford doesn't know about the photos of me and her husband, does she?"

"Not from me. Mind if I take a nap now?"

"No, go ahead." Angelica did mind. She wanted to find

out what else he knew, but minutes later, snores and whistles invaded the tranquility of the beach. At least, the mystery of the graffiti had been solved. She would have the scratches taken care of when she got her bumper fixed. Good news, at last.

While Dex slept, she studied the intricate silver cross on his upper left arm. His hair and eyebrows grew lighter as they dried in the sun. He wasn't bad looking, she decided, even though his eyes and teeth, his best features, were temporarily hidden. However, his nose looked the worse for wear. Perhaps he had played football in school and dated cheerleaders resembling Lindy Weiss—although she still didn't know what Bedford's girlfriend looked like from the front. She folded an arm beneath her head and, hypnotized by Dex's breathing, soon drifted into a deep sleep of her own.

Bare-chested astride a snowy stallion, blond hair streaming beneath a Viking helmet, Dex holds aloft a mighty sword and, sweeping the slender maiden onto the pommel, goads the steed forward, hooves stretching across the silver sand . . .

"Wakey, wakey," a voice chanted above her.

She blinked open her eyes.

"We best get moving," Dex told her. "I'm dying for a beer and you're beginning to look like a boiled lobster. There's bottled water under the seat of the WaveRunner, but it'll be lukewarm."

She stretched languidly while he stood and shook out his towel. "I had the strangest dream," she told him.

"Me too."

"You were a warrior who came to save me."

"From what?"

"I don't know. What was your dream about?"

"I was marooned here with Lindy Weiss."

Angelica scrambled to her feet and flapped the sand from

her towel in irritation. He was clearly obsessed with that woman. "Mind if I ask you something?" she said, following him to the WaveRunner. "Did you see tapes of Lindy Weiss with Peter Bedford?"

"Why d'you want to know?"

"Why do you always answer a question with a question?"

"Occupational hazard, I guess."

"Well, change occupation," Angelica retorted, flouncing off down the beach.

"I'm happy doing what I do," he called after her.

She whirled around on the sand. "What? Spying on people?"

Dex stared at her for a long moment. "I only did that for Bella as an extended service." He walked up to the water craft and pulled his life vest off the seat. "Her husband was cheating on her all over the place and she needed proof. Per a pre-nup, she wouldn't get much for herself or her kids if she left without cause."

"Well, she doesn't need to worry about that now, does she?"

"That depends on whether the police think she had anything to do with his death."

"You mean she might have hired someone to kill her husband?"

"The cops are looking into every possible scenario." Dex gazed at the water lapping his feet, blond tresses falling forward in thick ropes from his face.

"Your hair must be a pain to brush out," Angelica remarked.

He flung his arms through the holes of the orange vest. "You don't like it, do you?"

"I'm just envious, I guess."

"You needn't be." He reached out and tucked a loose strand of her hair behind her ear. "And by the way, I prefer brunettes."

Angelica felt her face glow beneath the sunburn. She felt tempted to take his strong hand in hers, but already he had withdrawn it and was buckling the straps on his life vest.

Perhaps he would ask her out to dinner that evening.

28

*D*ex had not invited her to dinner. Not that she really cared, she managed to persuade herself, but she felt safe with the private detective and found she trusted him. However, if it wasn't Dex spying on her at the pool, who was it? And who had sent her on the Fioretti listing appointment and pushed Bedford to his death? Just because Lindy Weiss had keyed her car didn't mean she was responsible for everything else, convenient as it was to assume.

At four o'clock, Angelica wandered into Jenn's cubicle to return her novel, which she had never finished after Bedford left his exploding gift at her door and scared her out of her wits. She could not find the sales associate. Come to think of it, Jenn had not been in the office since Friday, which was puzzling since, as a recently licensed agent, she never liked to miss floor duty as an opportunity for new leads. The first months were sink or swim in real estate unless you had savings or spousal support, and Jenn had neither, as far as Angelica knew.

A glance at Jenn's desk calendar showed several blank spaces, the last entry being Friday morning: *Scrob, #? Flamingo Circle, 11:00.* Angelica sat down at the desk and called her colleague's cell phone. After leaving a brief message, she tried her home number and breathed a sigh of relief when someone answered.

"Jenn?"

"No, it's Kim, her roommate."

"This is Angelica, from Plum Realty. Jenn's not been in for four days and hasn't called in sick."

"Last I saw her was Thursday evening," Jenn's roommate informed her. "She didn't tell me she had plans for the weekend, but she took off once before without saying anything. Her plants haven't been watered in days."

"Her family lives up in Jacksonville, right?"

"I called her parents. She's not there and she hasn't contacted them in over a week. I don't know what else to do."

Angelica gave Kim her cell phone number. "Call me if you hear from her. I know she had an appointment Friday, so I'll check that out first."

"Should we call the cops?"

Kim sounded worried, as well she should be, Angelica thought. Anything could have happened to Jenn. After assuring Kim she would call the police if there was still no news of Jenn by the end of the day, she searched for Rusty Scrob's number, only to discover that his phone was out of order, or else had been disconnected. She would have to drive to Flamingo Circle.

"I could cancel my date and come with you," Kathy offered when Angelica told her where she was going. "It's a bit fishy that Jenn disappeared around the time she was supposed to see Rusty Scrob, especially as you were both telling me how creepy he is. And it'll be dark when you get there."

Knowing that Kathy had been angling for a date with Phil from the office for months, Angelica said she would call Dex and ask him to escort her.

Kathy winked. "Good thinking. Great excuse to see him. And a private eye would be just the person to take along."

In spite of Angelica's description of him as several pounds

overweight, longhaired and tattooed, Kathy was all for the match. Opposites attract, she had reminded Angelica, who insisted it was a moot point since he hadn't called her since their return from Dragonfly Island. As she entered his number on her phone, she wondered what sort of reception she would get, but she got his voice mail and, like a teen with a crush, canceled the call at the end of his message.

She sat in her car without moving. Did she dare go to Rusty Scob's house alone? Perhaps she should call the police right away. But if Scrob had nothing to do with Jenn's disappearance, she would look like an even bigger fool to the detectives than she already did.

Broker Bob had warned her to stay away from the Scrob place. Well, she wouldn't. Something dark and mysterious drew her to Flamingo Circle. It was Jenn's last known destination. Armed with cell phone and pepper spray, and no real clue as to what she would do when she got there, Angelica started the car and drove north in the gathering dusk.

29

*P*arking a short distance from Scrob's property, Angelica cut her headlights. The house squatted in darkness, quiet as a morgue. The pick-up was gone, and she thought it safe to assume Scrob was not home, unless Florida Power & Light had disconnected his electricity—which might explain why his doorbell did not work. Her knock on the door echoed eerily. She waited. Nothing.

Retrieving a flashlight from her trunk, she followed its thin beam around the side of the bungalow, afraid the black pit bull would suddenly lunge at her from out of the shadows. Her beam revealed a colony of fire ant mounds in the unmowed grass where the green bathtub had been interred since her last visit and had begun to collect, per Scrob's master plan, a bottom full of rainwater. Tied to a rusty stake, a frayed rope lay coiled on the ground. Had Scrob vacated the premises, taking the dog with him? Angelica shone her beam into a window. A pair of yellow eyes stared back at her. Gasping with fright, she dropped the light.

As she bent to retrieve it, she felt a squashy object and promptly retracted her hand. On closer inspection, she discovered it was a woman's muddy shoe, pointed at the toe—a fashion that could only have been devised by a man to fulfill some sadistic foot fetish. More importantly, it looked like Jenn's shoe. That it was abandoned in Scrob's back yard while the rest of Jenn was missing set Angelica's neck hairs on end. What other evidence might she find? She had no time to find out. The crack of trodden palm fronds alerted her to another presence in the yard.

"'Ey!" unfurled a male voice full of unbred menace, followed by an ominous ratcheting sound. "It's you, ain't it? That *reelater*. I seed your car parked out front."

"I came to find Jenn," she stammered. "Your name was on her appointment calendar, and I thought she might be here."

"Well, she ain't."

"My mistake!" Angelica said with forced cheer.

Scrob's elastic form and the outline of a long-barreled gun gained definition as he approached. He put his fingers to his mouth and let out an ear-splitting whistle. "Guess I'll let ole Rebel take care of ya," he threatened. "Here, boy!"

Angelica froze in the weeds. Steps thudded up the driveway, chains rattled. Angelica let out a scream. A figure bathed in light burst into view. Macho Cop! Cavalry bugles played in her head.

"Lay your weapon on the ground, Rusty," the cop instructed, gun drawn, his other hand aiming his flashlight at Scrob.

"She's trespassin'!"

"We'll get to that in a moment. Right now, I need you to relinquish your firearm."

Scrob deposited his shotgun on the grass and straightened up in slow motion, hands in the air.

"That's good," the cop said. "Now, step closer to the woman so I can see you both. Okay, what's going on here? Ma'am, you seem familiar. Name, please."

"Angelica Lane. The homicide at Plovers Key?" Recognition flickered across the officer's Hollywood features. "My friend went missing Friday morning," she pressed on in haste. "Jenn Johnson is this man's listing agent. I found her shoe in his yard." She held up the pointed leather footwear.

Macho Cop beamed his light on Scrob's unshaven face. "How d'you explain that, Rusty?"

Scrob shielded his eyes. "Dunno," he said. "My dog brings back stuff all the time."

"And where is old Rebel?"

"Musta got free of his rope agin."

"Seems like every week one of your neighbors calls the station about your dog or some disturbance or other. And a convicted felon got no right to own a gun, you know that."

"I got a constitutional right to defend myself against *reelaters*. I fired her!" Scrob shook his fist at Angelica. "Ya think ya'll can come snoopin' round my yard—"

"I got one pair of handcuffs, and it's your lucky day, Rusty. You know the routine."

Cursing and spitting, Scrob turned his back while Macho Cop cuffed his wrists and Angelica stood by with a feeling of smug righteousness. Scrob's aunt had omitted to disclose that Rusty had priors. She would have to have a word with her.

"Whatcha gonna do about Ms. Busybody?" Scrob asked the cop.

"My colleague could be gagged and bound inside the house, or buried in the yard!" Angelica protested. "That tub wasn't in the ground when I was here before. Her body could be under it!"

Sniggering, Scrob shook his head in derision.

Macho Cop stared at the tub, clearly trying to figure out its purpose. "Is it a hot tub?"

"Nuh-uh! I ripped it outta my own house!"

Macho Cop grinned. "I wasn't accusing you of stealing—yet."

Angelica asked if they could check inside the property; she had seen a pair of yellow eyes at the window. Jenn's parents lived at the other end of the state, she explained, and she felt responsible for her colleague.

"Any objection?" Macho Cop asked Scrob.

"Hell yeah. There's only Charlene inside."

"Charlene?"

"My Burmese Python."

Angelica shivered. "Maybe we should get backup?"

"I can get a search warrant for the property, if necessary," Macho Cop replied. "In the meantime, why don't you come down the station in your car, Ms. Lane, and file a missing person's report."

She watched with relief as the police officer led Rusty Scrob to the cruiser. The felon was now safely in custody, but where was Jenn?

30

*D*ex called as she drove home from the police station. "Why didn't you leave a message when you phoned?" he asked. "Kathy Ellis from your office called to make sure I was going with you to Scrob's place since she couldn't accompany you herself."

Angelica felt gratified to hear a note of concern in his voice. "It's all taken care of," she said in a brisk tone designed to convey her cool headedness. "Rusty Scrob's in custody and the police are going to search his property."

"Who's he? And what makes you think your friend's there?"

"Just a hunch. No one's seen or heard from Jenn since she was supposed to go to his house on a listing appointment. And I found her shoe in his yard. I think Rusty Scrob may have killed before."

"Huh?"

"He's a convicted felon, and he mentioned a dead brother. The way he said it was creepy, like he had something to do with his death. And I spoke to his aunt just now. She was real cagey about what happened to her deceased nephew. Something about a leaky boat sinking in the Everglades, and a swamp buggy operator finding the remains of a body chewed up by alligators."

"Nice. How come you didn't take someone else from your office?"

Angelica laughed, mentally checking off Rick Powers, Broker Bob and old Bill Bungle. Phil was out on a date with Kathy, and Gloria would have worried about chipping her nail polish. "I don't think so," she replied. "And I thought some espionage would be right up your alley."

"What if this Scrob character had come at you with a gun?"

"He did come at me with a gun."

"What did you do?"

"I talked him down. And then someone must have called nine-one-one, because a cop turned up. The neighbors hate Scrob. I found out at the station that the Friends of Feathers Society came to rescue the chickens, and Pet Protective Services took the dog. Hopefully it can be rehabilitated. He has a Burmese Python as well."

"This guy sounds like a complete Froot Loop. And so do you, by the way. It was dumb to go over there on your own."

"Would you have come?"

"I would have told you to let the cops take care of it."

"Well, I don't have much faith in *them*," Angelica replied tartly. "They haven't gotten anywhere in the Bedford case."

"Says you."

"Yes, says me. Unless you can tell me different." She waited for a response. "Can you?"

"I can't."

"Or won't, you mean."

No answer.

Her brain froze as she tried to think of something to keep Dex on the phone. It was reassuring to speak with him after all the drama that evening. In spite of her bravado, she felt jittery. "Have you eaten yet?" she asked.

"What did you have in mind?"

"Pizza? A glass of wine perhaps?"

"I mean, why d'you want to see me?"

Why did he have to make this so difficult? "I'm just feeling a bit nervous about what happened—you know, with the gun?"

"You don't sound nervous."

"Well, I am. And I'm concerned about Jenn. I need someone to talk to, and Kathy's on a date. I'm incredibly upset."

"Okay then," he said. "Where?"

"Wherever you like!"

"It was your idea."

Angelica growled in frustration. "You know, Dex, you're about as uncooperative as a help desk in India."

"This is Brad," Dex took off in a singsong voice. "It is really Syed Patel, which is a dead giveaway—please to note the English idiom we learn in customer service class. And so how may I be helping you today? I have thirty flash cards, so you may get lucky. If you ask to speak with my supervisor, you will be disconnected, so very sorry, and will have to start all over again with pressing many-many buttons, which will be beyond annoying for you."

"Very funny," Angelica said through a smile. So Dex had a sense of humor. "Well, if pizza's okay with you, there's *La Dolce Vita* on Beach Road."

"Just one thing," he said. "I don't do dates."

"You what?"

"Since four years ago."

"What happened four years ago?"

"The girl I'd been with forever decided it was time to move on."

Angelica slowed down on the outer lane. "Are you saying you haven't been on a date in all that time?"

"I've been busy with work and rehabbing houses. I'm almost thirty-five and I don't need the aggravation."

Angelica ignored the honking horns behind her. "So we'll

meet at La Dolce Vita in fifteen minutes," she said firmly, as though closing an appointment. She wasn't about to let this rare specimen off the hook.

Throwing the car into a U-turn, she zoomed back up the highway, making it to the restaurant in ten. As the black SUV pulled up beside her, Angelica did a double-take. Dex wore a pressed white shirt, his hair bound in a smooth ponytail.

"You're wearing a tie," she said as he stepped out of the vehicle.

"Yah. I *can* look presentable when I need to." And he did look more than presentable—much to her shamed surprise. "I had a meeting," he explained.

"I hope you get overtime."

"Bosses don't get overtime," he said holding the restaurant door open for her.

"Table for two?" the hostess inquired.

She led them to a table tucked in an alcove and left them to peruse their menus. Just as they were deciding on a starter, Dex's cell phone signaled an incoming text.

"Oh, heck," he said, reading the message. "It's an emergency. Sorry, Angelica, I'm going to have to take a rain check on dinner. I wouldn't do this if it wasn't really important." He dropped a pile of bills on the table, pecked her on the cheek, and strode out of the restaurant.

Her heart sank into her Nine West pumps. Smiling bravely at the waitress, she asked if she could have a pizza to go. She wondered how Kathy's date was going with the gallant Phil. She suddenly felt very lonely. Her dad had Nuala, her sister had Sam. Her mother was remarried. It seemed everyone in the world had someone, except her.

31

*T*he next afternoon, Angelica sat brooding in her cubicle over the "emergency" that had whisked Dex away from the restaurant. She could not shake the feeling it had something to do with Lindy, who had been having an affair with Bedford and now appeared to have her claws in Dex.

She heard a preparatory cough in the adjoining cubicle as Fred punched numbers into his desk phone.

"Mrs. Mortimer? Great news!" he dove in, working off a Century 21 telesales script. "I'm Fred Schnauzer and I can help you sell your home! Isn't that gr-reat?" Angelica cringed in her chair. "But Plum Realty can sell it quicker than you can on your own . . . Believe me, Mrs. Mortimer," Fred boomed through the partition, "Your husband will thank you! Does he work regular hours? . . . Purr-fect. I have an opening this evening. Would seven or eight work better for you? Wait!" *Click* of phone. "Dumb FSBO's," he muttered.

A second later, Angelica heard the crumple of brown paper, the rasp of a metal top being unscrewed, a glug of liquid, and a relieved expulsion of breath as Tony the Tiger hit the vodka again. If she wasn't careful, she could end up as burned-out as poor Fred. She swore then and there never to let work turn her into an addict, forever fixated on the next sale and losing track of what was going on in her personal life. What personal life? Her family was scattered to the four winds, and Dex hadn't made it past the minestrone.

With a heavy sigh, she headed for reception. Kathy had taken off for root canal surgery that afternoon, and Angelica had offered to fill in at the front desk. There Rick informed her that old Bill Bungle had made a sale that day, the first in two years. "Proving the theory that even a blind squirrel can find a nut," he added uncharitably.

These days Rick sported designer stubble and looked like a guy model on a Guess? ad. Kathy called it his Clean Grunge Phase.

"That is so callous," Angelica told him. She had not been in a good mood to begin with. "And what's more, I think this race for Bill's office before his chair is even cold is totally inappropriate."

"The competition is supposed to make us more productive," a bleary-eyed Fred grumbled as he plodded toward the front door.

"Plum Realty has been around longer than most independent offices, so Broker Bob must be doing something right," Rick pointed out, preening his perfect hair in the reflection of his cell phone.

"He micromanages more than most," Angelica retorted, taking Kathy's seat and reaching for the ringing phone on the desk.

The caller inquired about her Palm Meadow listing, but as soon as she informed him of the price, he hung up before she could interest him in comparable properties. Afterward, she signed on as a guest on Kathy's Internet Service Provider and keyed in her password. *You've got mail,* the electronic voice congratulated her. Embedded in her inbox, a message from Dexter Home Security leaped out at her. Her heart skipping a beat, she clicked on *Read,* and a short message popped onto the screen.

Hey, sorry about last night. Things are crazy right now but we'll do the dinner thing soon, okay? Goth Biker

Her face broke into a smile. She liked the intimacy implied in the "we," and the way he signed off was cute, too. It was like their own private joke. However, he had stood her up at the restaurant, and for that reason alone she was tempted to leave his email unanswered.

A minute later, she reconsidered and started typing paragraphs about how much she disliked first dates herself, how she knew she was supposed to play hard-to-get, but what a waste of time *that* was, and how men hesitated to ask her out because she wasn't the flirty type, and she felt constrained with men a lot of the time, probably because her mother had always insisted she be a good girl, and most guys didn't go for good girls in the twenty-first century, except for losers and, let's face it, creeps like Rick at the office who chased anything with two X chromosomes . . .

Deleeeeete.

"Okay," she wrote instead, signing herself "Avon Lady" and, after a brief hesitation, pressing *Send.*

Rick hovered by the reception desk, laptop bag slung over his shoulder. "It's almost six," he said. "Want to get a drink?"

"Thanks, I think I'll pass."

"Anybody heard from Jenn?" he asked.

"Not yet, but the police are looking into her disappearance. Look, sorry about my outburst about Bill's office. It's just that scary things are happening to people I know, and it makes our squabbles at work seem pretty petty."

"No problem. Have a good night. And regards to Mighty Mutt," Rick added as he left.

Very funny, she thought, visualizing the dog waiting for her, impatient for his walk. She shut down the computer and locked the front door behind her, the crown logo of Plum

Realty, Inc. Co. etched in gold in the unwashed glass. At the tip of each prong of the crown balanced a ball containing a company initial, creating the acronym P.R.I.C.

Angelica felt compelled at that moment to finger in the letter K, as an insult to Broker Bob for suggesting a vacation until the Bedford saga blew over.

"Miss Lane?"

Wheeling around, Angelica found herself face to face with a silver-haired man in a tailored suit, his craggily handsome features as though hewn from granite.

"Yes?" she replied, hoping he hadn't witnessed her childish prank.

"I apologize for accosting you like this," he said, holding out his hand. "I'm Paul Johnson, Jenn's father."

Angelica eagerly took the proffered hand. The situation must indeed be serious if Jenn's dad had come down from Jacksonville. Perhaps Mr. Johnson had news.

32

*"H*ave you heard from her?" Angelica blurted, feeling the weight of responsibility lift from her shoulders now that Mr. Johnson was in town to take over the search for his daughter.

He shook his head. "No news, I'm afraid. That's why I'm here. Do you have a moment?" He indicated a garnet red Mercedes sedan whose hood ornament twinkled in the late afternoon sun. "A friend loaned me his house in Portofino. Would you mind coming over to speak with my wife? Naturally, she's distraught."

"Of course I don't mind," Angelica said, slipping into the passenger seat with her briefcase while Mr. Johnson held open the door.

The leather smelled new. She had not expected Jenn's parents to be this well-off, but everything about Paul Johnson bespoke elegance, from his heavy gold cuff links to his supple kidskin shoes.

"Are you and Jennifer close?" he asked as he fastened his seatbelt.

"Well, we're friends, although we don't see much of each other outside work. But then, Jenn hasn't been with Plum Realty that long, as you know."

Mr. Johnson concentrated on finding a break in the traffic. "You're the Realtor that got mixed up in that unfortunate business at Plovers Key, right?" he asked as the luxury sedan glided onto the highway.

"Yes," she replied, wondering if the story had reached Jacksonville.

"It must have been a shock for you. Did you know your client well?"

"Not that well. But Peter Bedford seemed like a nice man." What else could she say about her dead client? That he made exploding gifts and had tried to seduce her at every opportunity?

"And do you like real estate, Ms. Lane?"

"Well, I did until that happened."

Mr. Johnson smiled tightly. "I can well imagine."

As they crossed town, he asked why she had chosen a career in real estate. Angelica explained that her mother used to take her to open houses, and she had grown up with an appreciation for architecture and interior design. She refrained from adding that they could never afford such homes on her dad's military pay, even if they had been able to stick around long enough to enjoy them. Her mom had finally found someone who could buy one for her. "My mother has a beautiful new house in Portland and is very happy," she told Mr. Johnson.

"Physical surroundings have little to do with real happiness," he said sententiously.

Angelica cast an eye over the plush interior of the Benz and nodded without conviction.

Ten minutes later, they sailed through the residents' gate of the St. Croix Golf & Country Club. The date palms planted at the entrance lent an exotic feel, as did the profusion of subtropical flowering shrubs adorning the median between the brick paved roads. In the distance beyond custom built homes Angelica glimpsed undulations of green turf traversed by golf carts. At the clubhouse, an Italianate affair with a multi-tiered roof and a profusion of porticoes, valet attendants wearing white gloves opened the doors of expensive cars lining up outside the grand entrance.

"Do you play golf?" Angelica asked Mr. Johnson.

"When time permits," he replied, seeming distracted.

He must be worried about Jenn, she concluded, and wondered what her colleague's mother, whom she was about to meet, was like.

At the end of a maze of streets they entered a new enclave with a sign welcoming them to Verona. At the end of a cul-de-sac they turned into a driveway leading to a set of mahogany gates blocking all but the top of a russet barrel-tile roof from view. To the side of the entrance, a triple-door garage peeled back, and Mr. Johnson parked between a Rolls Silver Shadow and a Lamborghini Diablo.

"Your briefcase will be safe in the car," he told Angelica. "We won't keep you long."

She followed him through a door in the garage to a cobbled courtyard adorned with clay urns and classical nude statues missing various appendages. A school of koi streaked through a pebble-bottomed pond. Angelica was amazed to discover her nondescript colleague had such wealthy contacts. And then, quite suddenly, Jenn herself appeared, dressed in a pink silk gown, her face expressionless as she crossed the decorative stone bridge spanning the pond. Just as suddenly, Jenn's father turned on Angelica.

"Look out!" she heard Jenn scream as, snatching Angelica's purse, he strode back toward the door to the garage.

"Ms. Johnson," he said, hand poised on the handle. "Perhaps you can show Angelica Lane around the property. By the way, the Dior looks lovely on you." Next, he addressed Angelica. "To repeat what I already told Ms. Johnson: If you breach any exit points, my security detail will be alerted and you will come to grievous bodily harm."

Angelica gave a start. Peter Bedford had come to grievous bodily harm.

The man swept an arm within the sunkissed confines of the courtyard. "Please enjoy your stay." And so saying, he slipped through the door.

Angelica raced after him. The door slammed in her face, followed by a resounding snap of the lock. Seconds later, a car engine roared to life.

The entire episode had lasted mere minutes.

"I'm so glad you're here!" Jenn cried, throwing herself into Angelica's arms. "I couldn't believe it when I saw you. I'd given up hope."

Bewildered, Angelica pulled away. "What's going on?" She put a hand to her temple, her head in a spin.

"You heard what that—that man said. All the exterior doors and windows are fitted with alarms. The garage doors are reinforced metal and the gates are three-inch solid wood. We're prisoners!"

"But he claimed to be your father," Angelica protested.

"I never saw him before he kidnapped me six days ago! He brought me here on the pretext of putting the property on the market. I never thought . . ."

Angelica hugged her sobbing colleague. She knew the feeling. Sometimes the desire to make a sale could wipe out common sense. Not that she had shown much sense herself, having gullibly stepped into a stranger's car.

"I think he means to kill us," Jenn wailed.

"Nonsense. Just watch me walk out those gates."

Jenn held her back. "You can't. They're rigged with alarms. The man's goons will come after us. Don't you understand? We can't escape!"

The solid mahogany gates loomed above them, blocking their way to freedom. Jenn wept openly as she described how she had been left all alone and afraid.

33

*D*rying her eyes, Jenn pulled herself together. "Let me show you around," she said with a sniffle. "As you can see, the courtyard design affords complete privacy—"

"And secrecy," Angelica pointed out with growing dismay. The pretend Mr. Johnson could be serious about imprisoning them there. No one could see in.

"Note the Tuscan architecture and limestone accents. The main house and twin guest cabanas comprise a total of seven thousand square feet under air—"

"I don't need a guided tour," Angelica remonstrated. "We've got to find a way out of here! Why didn't you call someone?"

"There's no working phone line, and I left my cell in the man's car."

Realizing that she, too, had left her phone in his car, Angelica tore through the arched entranceway to the main part of the house and into an airy foyer. Plunging down a marble hall hung with teardrop chandeliers, she passed numerous doors and eventually found the one to the garage.

The Mercedes stood there, regal and still, the Rolls had gone. Peering through the window of the Benz, she saw that her briefcase and cell phone were not where she had left them. He must have taken them with him. She and Jenn had no contact with the outside world. For all the luxury of their surroundings, they might as well be locked up in San

Quentin. Then she remembered Hercules. She had filled his water bowl that morning and left him dry food, but he would run out in a day. Don't panic, she told herself. There must be a solution.

"Are you sure you searched the whole house?" she quizzed her colleague.

"I spent the first two days looking for a way out. It's hopeless."

"Any laptops?"

Jenn shook her head dispiritedly.

"Let's try again, just the same," Angelica said gently.

Her colleague responded with a droop of the shoulders. This was not the eager-beaver Angelica knew from the office. But then, Jenn had been alone for almost a week with no one to talk to. Angelica speculated on the reason they had been brought to this house. Was their kidnapper planning to keep them out of the way for some reason, or did he intend to do away with them altogether? Their abduction must have something to do with Bedford's murder, but where did Jenn fit in? So much to think about, and time was against them.

In the courtyard, shadows lengthened the shapes of the urns and statues, the warmth of the evening sun trapped within the walls, just as they were trapped.

"Help!" she yelled at the top of her lungs. "Help." Her words echoed forlornly. She kept at it until she was hoarse.

"There's no one to hear us," Jenn said. "I even put the sound system on at full volume hoping someone would come by and complain, but nobody did."

Angelica assessed the high blocks of stone draped with red and purple bougainvillea. "Why don't we scale the walls?"

"No!" Jenn restrained her by the arm. "The magno-electric fields at the top will electrocute anyone who tries to climb over." With a languid gesture, she indicated a mitered window above a rectangular pool of sparkling blue water. "That's the library. You should see the ceiling. It's painted like the Sistine Chapel."

Angelica contemplated Jenn's wistful face. "I wish it was your listing, I really do. And that I was just here to preview."

"That's how he got me here!" Jenn interjected. "He said he was Eric Forbes, or someone, and that I'd come highly recommended. He asked me to step into his car to discuss listing his estate home. Here was this clean-cut older guy driving a Rolls. I didn't think twice. I just hopped in, thinking, Wow, St. Croix, that's like the most upscale golf community in Portofino. Anyway, he showed me around and asked if I would be happy staying here for a few days while he took a trip abroad. He said it would be a good way for me to get acquainted with the house. I thought, Great, and asked him when he wanted me to house-sit, and he said immediately. I told him I had to get some clothes and make arrangements with my roommate, and he said there were clothes in the closet and everything I could possibly need in the house. I thought, like, this guy's a bit eccentric, but he's rich and probably used to getting his own way, so I thought, Fine, I'll just go and pick up my stuff when he leaves. I asked about transportation because, of course, I didn't have my car, and he said not to worry, I could use any car in the garage, and I thought, Cool."

"But you couldn't, of course."

Jenn shook her head, her nervous energy depleted. "The garage doors won't open and I can't find the car keys."

Angelica couldn't believe how naive they had been, but what was done was done, and now she and Jenn had to try and fix it. However, as they continued their search through the spacious rooms it became apparent that nowhere afforded any clues as to the owner's identity or any means of escape.

34

*I*n the library, drawers and cabinets gaped open, empty but for a lone paperclip. No identifying records existed, not even a phone bill. It was as impersonal as a room in a model home, except for a framed black-and-white photo of a woman in a strapless gown and black gloves to the elbows, her blonde hair styled in a sixties' bouffant. The picture *could* be a more recent glamour shot, Angelica surmised, replacing it on the tooled leather desk.

Floor-to-ceiling shelves filled with leather-bound volumes dressed the walls, accessed by a librarian's ladder attached to a rail.

"Oh, look!" Jenn cried, picking a book off the shelf. "Rebekkah Stein's acclaimed debut novel, *Demise in Paradise*. It's an 'erotical,' a new genre of historical," Jenn explained. She proceeded to read out the back cover blurb. " 'Sisters Issy and Lily, London socialites of the 1700s, are captured by pirates on a sea voyage to the Carolinas. Abandoned on a deserted Caribbean island, they await their terrible fate.' "

Angelica winced, thinking: That could be us.

Jenn tucked the book in the crook of her arm, a look of joyful anticipation illuminating her face. Clearly she had forgotten their predicament, or else was choosing to ignore it. Angelica began to fear for her colleague's sanity. Solitary confinement, even in a luxury home, could cause psychological problems, she reasoned.

Jenn showed her the last part of the house. They stood on the threshold gazing into the master suite. Beneath a mirrored ceiling a circular bed piled high with cushions dominated the room. Jenn sank down on the embroidered damask comforter, and the bed began to revolve at a sedate pace. Angelica imagined it speeding up, the occupants flung out by centrifugal force and landing splat on the glazed rose walls. She began to feel giddy just watching.

"Wait until you see all the clothes," Jenn declared, rising from the bed. She threw open a run-around closet, one entire wall fitted with pigeonhole shelving accommodating strappy Jimmy Choo stilettos, sequined Blahnik sandals, and Ferragamo and Yves Saint Laurent pumps. "Aren't these to die for?"

Not so much, Angelica thought. Jenn must be delusional. How could she say such a thing?

That was just the shoes.

Donna Karin and Dolce & Gabbana suits, Trussardi summer dresses, and Chanel and Versace evening wear succeeded each other willy-nilly on racks. There were, in addition, beautiful bold creations by Vera Wang and Diane von Furstenberg, and bags for every occasion by Gucci, Klein, and other top designers, all heaped in a corner.

How could someone so label-conscious be such a slob? Angelica wondered. And who was this spoiled diva anyway?

In stark contrast, the closet opposite was empty except for a handful of hangers still wrapped in plastic from the dry cleaner's. The door to a safe built into the wall hung open, the contents cleared out, leaving it bare.

Off the dressing room, a bathroom gleamed with opulent marble, the focal point an overflow feature whirlpool tub reposing on a pedestal. Within viewing distance of the bath, a television screen defaulted to a reproduction of Botticelli's *Birth of Venus.* Towels with gold fringes, exotic bath oils, and lavender-scented soap from Provence graced each scallop shell basin set in a pair of vanities accessorized with gold-plated knobs. In a corner, two massage tables covered with white terrycloth lay side by side.

Angelica followed Jenn to a tunneled shower equipped with dual showerheads, each with its own computerized temperature control. The glass wall overlooked a garden adorned with pagoda bridges and topiaries in the shape of peacocks and swans.

Jenn pressed a panel and the glass slid apart, exposing the shower to the elements. "Very Zen, don't you think?"

Pools filled with koi and lily pads formed a series of interconnecting pods that gave the illusion of flowing beneath the house to join the pond in the courtyard.

"No one can see us because of the privacy wall," Angelica lamented, returning to the reality of their predicament. "And yet someone must maintain the shrubs."

"I haven't seen anyone, and the service gate is locked," Jenn said.

Angelica was not ready to give up, even if their kidnapper seemed to have thought of everything. Either he was a stickler for privacy or he had purposefully found a house so architecturally isolated that a person could be hidden away forever. Forever, she repeated to herself. That was the worrying part—not knowing how long they would be here or what might happen to them if the owner decided to curtail their stay.

After completing the tour, they shuffled into the kitchen, where a glass door led to a sundeck built over a manmade lake at the back of the house. Angelica reached for the knob.

"Don't open it!" Jenn cried. "See that flashing red light?"

Fear clamped Angelica in its steely grip. Backing away, she stared out at the view with deep longing. Her family might never find out what had happened to her. She would never discover Claire's secret or be able to tell her mother she understood her better now, the need for security that had driven her to leave Dad and marry someone boring like Dave. She'd never be able to tell her father she missed him more than anyone, especially now.

35

Angelica opened the top-of-the-line fridge-freezer. "Is that Brie?" she asked with determined cheerfulness. She had lost count of the rooms and needed something to eat to keep up her strength.

"There's caviar as well. It goes very well with the 1986 Taittinger Blanc de Blancs." From a door compartment Jenn produced a beeping champagne bottle. "This gadget tells you when the champagne has reached optimum temperature. Could you grab a couple of flute glasses from the Butler's Pantry?"

Angelica was amazed to see her colleague as busy as she was at the office. The office? What a remote memory that seemed all of a sudden. They had explored every nook and cranny of the property and were no closer to getting out of it.

As Jenn expertly popped the cork, a smoky wreath escaped from the bottle. "If we run out of this, there are crates of Cristal and pink Moët & Chandon in the cellar," she said, filling their glasses.

Angelica took thirsty gulps of the ice cold champagne, her stomach instantly imbued with delicious warmth. She began to wonder how much of the stuff Jenn had drunk before she arrived. The bubbly might help explain her strange behavior. Jenn had veered from a numb state of shock to one bordering on hysteria, and Angelica didn't quite know what to make of it. Rummaging in the refrigerator, she pulled out a jar of artichoke hearts and a small sealed terrine of *pâté de foie gras*. From the freezer she selected a chocolate-marbled cheesecake, which she set out on the counter to thaw. After all, they should have something extra to soak up the alcohol while they considered their options.

In the pantry, she found jars of spaghetti sauce, tins of gourmet soup, and an array of musical-sounding pasta. At least they wouldn't starve in a hurry. She hunted through the cabinets for plates and silverware. "Are there any sharp knives?" she asked Jenn, who stood rinsing grapes at the granite-top center island beneath a rack of stainless steel pans and colanders.

"You'll be disappointed if you're thinking of using a weapon. Our abductor was very methodical about removing anything that might aid us in defending ourselves."

Angelica inspected the serrated edge of the single large kitchen knife she could find. "Not much use unless we plan to saw him," she remarked as cartoon images of bloodless death and destruction flashed through her mind. She carried the laden silver tray through to the family room, while Jenn trailed after her with an ice bucket.

Her colleague lolled on a white leather sofa set at right angles to the one Angelica sat on. "You know, I envy you, Angelica," she said. "You always seem so together. Like now—and the way you handle yourself at work. You don't let Broker Bob get to you. And you act so cool with Rick."

"That's not an act. I really can't stand him."

"I think he's cute," Jenn crooned, twiddling the stem of her glass.

Angelica's thoughts turned to Dex. Had he responded to her email? She derived a measure of grim satisfaction from imagining him wonder why he never heard from her again.

Jenn helped herself to more champagne. "What do you

think will happen to us?"

"Don't worry," Angelica said. "If our abductor wanted to do something to us, he'd have done it already instead of letting us drink though his stock of vintage champagne."

"You think?" Jenn stroked away a tear. "I'm so happy you're here, Angelica."

"Well, I'm not, although I am glad to see you're okay. When I found your shoe, I thought Scrob had done something horrible to you."

"What shoe? I was about to go to his house when the guy in the Rolls approached me and brought me here."

"I wonder what would happen if we cut the electricity." Angelica looked around the living room where table lamps cast reassuring pools of light over the elegant Ethan Allen furniture. "But I suppose the alarm system works independently."

Jenn hiccupped. "Yeah, and the circuit breaker box is locked up tight, just like everything else."

Angelica let Jenn top up her glass and raised it in a toast, entranced by the golden bubbles shooting to the surface. "Here's to living it up at the Hotel Verona," she said, reaching out to clink glasses. "And to escaping soon."

In the meantime, all they could do was make the most of it. Arranging herself more comfortably on the supple leather sofa, she encountered something cold and hard stuffed down the side of the squab, and fished out a familiar-looking gold watch. "It's Peter Bedford's," she exclaimed. "His initials are engraved on the back. I wonder what it's doing down the back of the sofa?"

"Maybe he was making out with our host's wife."

Angelica sat bolt upright, spilling her drink. "The photograph in the library could be of the blonde at Plovers Key! That's the motive for murder! Bedford was having an affair with the killer's wife!"

"But why bring *us* here?"

Angelica flopped back on the cushions. "I don't know. My head's spinning." A loud clunk startled her, and she jumped, spilling the rest of her champagne. "What was that?" she croaked. "Did you hear it?"

Jenn, panic-stricken, stared in the direction of the kitchen. "Shhh," she whispered. "I think someone's back there. What are we gonna do?"

Angelica's first reaction was to hide, but where? She grabbed a poker from beside the carved fake log fireplace and, heart pounding in her throat, crept toward the living room doors. She heard Jenn behind her and, glancing over her shoulder, saw her armed with an onyx bookend in the form of an elephant.

She led the way down the hall to the kitchen where they had left the ceiling lights blazing. The vast space afforded nowhere to hide except in the broom closet or Butler's Pantry. A stairway by the back door to the deck led to a partial upper floor housing a gym and a media room. Someone could have bolted up there when they heard them approach. She glanced at Jenn whose hands trembled beneath the weight of the bookend. Suddenly, the clunk sounded again, much louder. Angelica spun around. Jenn dropped the elephant, which cracked on the stone tile. The noise had come from the massive fridge-freezer.

"It's the ice-maker," Jenn gasped, doubling over in relief.

Gripping the edge of the center island, Angelica shut her eyes and let out a long breath.

"Can we share the master suite tonight?" Jenn asked, her mournful brown eyes reminding Angelica of Hercules.

Angelica agreed. She, too, would feel safer if they stayed together. Just because they couldn't leave the house didn't mean nobody could come in at any time of the day or night. "I'm going to go soak in the tub, try and unwind," she told

Jenn. "Can you keep a look-out?"

She lit the main lights on her way, dispelling corners of shadow. Night clung to the French doors of the master bedroom leading onto the courtyard. She drew the pooled gossamer drapes. On the reproduction Louis XV chest of drawers stood a domed obelisk made of lustrous purple molded plastic, a foot tall. The base had a screw cap, presumably to adjust wattage, but when she touched it, the object started vibrating. As though electrocuted, her fingers flew open, and it fell to the carpet where it continued to buzz disconcertingly.

She observed the bed with misgivings. Had Jenn changed the sheets when she first arrived? Angelica imagined Bedford and the blonde on the bed, entangled limbs reflected in the circular mirror. But for Bedford she would never have gotten into this mess!

She squeezed a pillow to her chest. She had not felt this afraid since she was a child waking up in the dark, calling out for her father. "No monsters to report," he would say, striking a salute upon completing a thorough search of the bedroom. After her parents divorced, she had performed the monster check for Claire. Angelica smiled at the memory, even as it left a raw lump in her throat.

Conquering her fear, she padded across the plush carpet to the bathroom and filled the marble whirlpool tub, adding bubble bath from a small cut-glass bottle in the shape of a heart. Foam accumulated into icebergs of white cotton candy while a sensuous scent of rose essence wafted into the steam. Soaking in the fragrant bubbles, she aimed the remote at the television screen and turned on the power, only to encounter blur and static. They couldn't even watch the news to see if the police had launched a search. She began to suspect Jenn was right: Their situation was hopeless. No one looking for her and Jenn could possibly find them. They had disappeared without a trace.

36

*T*he next morning, Angelica awoke to find Jenn dead to the world, her face crushed against the silk pillow case, mouth half open. Angelica felt in no hurry to get up either. It had taken her hours to fall asleep the night before, and when she finally did, troubled dreams beset her. Stretching her toes beneath the smooth sheets, she recalled one particular dream where the photo in the library had come to life in a bizarre collage of images that even in sleep she had struggled to make sense of and now barely remembered.

If the woman in the gilt frame was the kidnapper's wife, it would explain why Bedford took her for clandestine sessions at the Plovers Key condo. Being married himself, that was a doubly dangerous game to play, but then her client had enjoyed dangerous games. Angelica's eyes strayed up to the mirror, hardly recognizing herself in the cream moiré silk negligee amid ripples of pale gold sheet. What had Bedford seen in her? And yet, viewing herself out of context like this, she saw reflected back at her a delicately boned brunette with sleek hair flowing onto the pillow, resembling an advertisement in a magazine.

Focus, focus, she reminded herself. She had to get out of here and return home to feed Herx. She rolled over and reached for the wall switch. The drapes opened, revealing a sunny courtyard abloom with orange honeysuckle and the purple of Golden Dewdrop. Tawny butterflies and ruby-throated humming birds hovered around the rampant clematis. On such a heavenly morning it hardly seemed possible that she and Jenn were being held captive. The idea was preposterous. And where was Dex when she needed him? She wished she hadn't insisted he stop following her. Had he even tried to get in touch with her, and if so, wouldn't he find her disappearance suspicious coming as it did on top of Jenn's?

Did he care?

Who else might report her missing? When Kathy saw her white Camry abandoned in the office parking lot, she would make inquiries . . . unless she was still at home recuperating from her dental operation.

"Oh, Angelica," Jenn mumbled, smiling sleepily. "It's so good to see you after waking up every morning and wondering if I was ever going to see another living soul again. And then dreading seeing you-know-who."

"Listen, Jenn, we really should give serious thought to how to escape."

Her friend sat up and shook out her mousy hair. "What do you suggest?"

"What about the roof?"

"You mean, climb onto it? How?"

"The ladder from the library."

"It's not tall enough. Besides, nobody comes into this neighborhood. At least, not to the end of the cul-de-sac. I never hear any cars."

"We only need one person to see our distress signal. A construction worker or someone walking their dog. It's worth a try. Did you see any paint or rope?"

Jenn shook her head. "We looked everywhere yesterday for anything that might be useful, remember. Every closet, every crawl space."

Angelica threw off the sheet and slipped into a pair of

sling-back pumps with a faux diamond stud nestled in the purple feathers.

"Anyway, who's going to go up the ladder?" Jenn asked. "I'm scared of heights. And it was your idea."

Angelica had to admit this was true.

"So you go up the ladder while I hold it," Jenn said.

All right then, Angelica thought. If risking her neck was what it took to get Jenn motivated, so be it. No time to change out of her negligee; best go now before her friend changed her mind. At least Jenn was wearing pajamas, blue satin ones, and more sensible slippers.

After managing to disengage the ladder from the rail in the library, they maneuvered it into the courtyard. Propped against the pale ochre stucco, it fell short of even the lowest portion of the roof.

"What now?" Jenn inquired.

"Let's see if we can hook it into the gutter. Once I'm up, I might be able to get down the other side and go for help. Ready? Lift."

"I can't feel my arms anymore," Jenn groaned as they balanced the ladder above their shoulders.

"One, two, three. Hold steady!"

The hooks grated against the gutter. Suddenly, the ladder lurched away from the wall, taking the women with it. They staggered about the courtyard with six feet of dead weight towering above their heads, Angelica tripping over the French lace trim of her nightgown.

"Back! Back!" she yelled, gasping with relief when this time the ladder held. "Here goes."

Jumping up, she curled her fingers around the highest rung she could reach and began hoisting herself up with her hands. Her weight proved too much. The gutter dipped and she clung on for dear life, suspended in her silk negligee, purple-feathered slippers perched on the tips of her toes.

Jenn shrieked as the gutter collapsed, sending Angelica into a clump of ferns. Extricating her from beneath the ladder, Jenn helped her into the master bedroom and eased her onto the bed.

By the time she returned with a cold compress, the bump on the back of Angelica's head had swollen to the size of a kumquat.

"There is one other thing that might work," Jenn ventured, chewing on her pinky nail. "How about we start a fire in the courtyard, to attract attention?"

"That's a great idea! If the blaze gets out of hand, there's plenty of water around." Angelica lifted her head from the pillow. "Ouch!"

"You need to rest first. I'll make us some brunch."

Prostrate on the bed, Angelica considered Jenn's plan from every angle. They would have to hope the fire trucks showed up before their abductor's cronies, whom the pretend Mr. Johnson had threatened would dispense grievous bodily harm on their persons.

When the throbbing in her head began to ease, she coaxed herself off the bed. An enticing aroma of freshly ground coffee wafted down the hall from the kitchen.

"Croissants?" Jenn offered, pulling a box from the freezer.

When her colleague turned around, Angelica's jaw dropped to the stone tile, her surprise at Jenn's transformation quite preventing her from uttering any sound remotely resembling speech. She simply stared. And stared some more.

37

Jenn had changed into a sleeveless, fawn-colored sweater by Prada, so sheer that her small pert breasts showed subtly through the silken cashmere. An Oscar de la Renta skirt in fuchsia suede, which Angelica had likewise admired in a copy of *Vogue,* hung low on Jenn's model thin hips, revealing her bellybutton. Her friend's hair, gleaming with a curried sheen, was parted to one side, helping to disguise the irregularity of her features, while the hot pink shade of lipstick managed to set off her sallow complexion to advantage. Silver hoop earrings and a pair of perilously high silver sandals that made her legs look as long as a stork's completed the metamorphosis of Jenn into a bona fide fashionista.

"G-goodness, Jenn," Angelica managed to stutter at last. "I might never have recognized you if you weren't the only other person in the house."

"Well, there's no excuse, is there? We've got tons of makeup, a warehouse full of clothes, and an endless supply of women's magazines."

Endless. Nothing was without end, except infinity, Angelica reflected. If they stayed long enough, they would come to the end of their supplies. They would run out of food and champagne. They would have to eat plants and hope they were not poisonous, or else resort to the koi. And then what?

"What's the matter?" Jenn asked. "You look pale. Do you

want another ice pack?"

"I just need to sit down for a minute."

Angelica unglued her eyes from the disconcerting vision of Jenn arranging butter in a dish of chipped ice. She was beginning to look a little too much at home in the *haute-cuisine* appointed kitchen. In fact, this could be a scene out of a remake of *The Stepford Wives* with Jenn playing the star zombie. Was she resigned to their fate or else in denial?

"Could you grab the plum preserve?" her friend asked.

Angelica picked up the jar. "This was made in Tiptree, England," she read off the label, at the same time reflecting that Great Britain could have been nuked off the face of the earth for all they knew. None of the televisions worked, and no computer had been left in the house.

The in-built microwave beeped, signaling that the croissants were ready. Angelica took the breakfast cups to a table in a shaded corner of the courtyard. With a simultaneous splash, the koi in the pond converged at her feet in a kaleidoscope of color.

"They're hungry," Jenn said, setting down the tray. "You'll find fish food in the summer kitchen."

The outdoor living area contained a vast gas grill and wicker furniture arranged around a wood-burning fireplace, ideal for entertaining in cooler weather. Entertaining whom? Angelica wondered. The place was deserted, the land version of a ghost ship.

She returned with the fish food and threw a pinch of granules into the water. The koi darted to the surface, snapping up the food in the blink of an eye. As she replaced the cap on the tube, a name caught her attention. "Look at this," she told Jenn. "Exotica Fish Food, a subsidiary of Forbes Biopharmaceuticals. Didn't you say the kidnapper's name was Forbes?"

"Do you always read the labels on everything?"

"Bedford said his colleague owned a pet food company. I bet you anything this is his house." Angelica slowly stirred a teaspoonful of sugar into her coffee. "I suppose it would make sense that Bedford was spending time here while his wife was in New York. Rather than going to a hotel, I mean."

Bella, as Angelica recalled, had not wanted anyone staying at the condo, anxious to keep it in pristine condition for a quick sale. And yet, if Bedford had been here, what had happened to his personal effects? Had Bella sent for them, or had they been hurriedly disposed of? And what of Forbes' possessions? All that remained of a personal nature were women's clothes and cosmetics. And the photo in the library.

"Well, I hope our being here isn't a prelude to us getting murdered, too," Jenn remarked, a shadow passing over her expertly made-up face. "I can understand Forbes wanting you out the way because of your connection to Bedford. But why me?"

Angelica appraised Jenn's slim build and mid-length hair. "I think he brought you here thinking you were me. He might have seen my picture in the paper or on one of my business cards at the condo. Then, when he realized his mistake, he kidnapped me as well."

"It's possible," Jenn agreed, reaching for another croissant. "He seemed to know who I was, so it's not like I had to introduce myself. And then he drove me straight here from the office."

"Your car wasn't in the parking lot."

Jenn stared back at her, and Angelica could tell something had clicked in her friend's brain. "My car's in the shop," Jenn told her. "I rented a Camry."

"What color?"

"White."

"Why did you get a car like mine?"

"I don't know," Jenn said meekly. "I suppose, deep down, I want to be just like you."

"Not so smart, Sunshine."

"But what do you have on this guy that he would go to the trouble of kidnapping you?"

"I don't know, other than that I was probably the last person besides the killer to see Bedford alive. Maybe Forbes thought I knew something incriminating. But I already told the police everything I know."

"Perhaps he plans to keep us hostage until he's safely out of the country."

"How's he going to release us if he's out of the country?"

The women exchanged looks of desperation.

"Look, maybe Forbes isn't the murderer after all," Angelica consoled Jenn. "Bella Bedford could have killed her husband. After all, she suspected he was being unfaithful and she had secret cameras set up in the condo."

"What have you gotten us mixed up in?"

"Obviously I didn't know about any of this when I took the listing, although, looking back, it does seem strange how enthusiastic she was about hiring me. I thought at first it was because of my presentation. I had no idea she had ulterior motives and that I was bait for her husband. Anyway, we're wasting time. I think we should get Plan B under way."

While Jenn hurried off to fetch paper, Angelica retrieved the lighter from the summer kitchen. Together they tore into books from the library, Angelica feeling a twinge of guilt as she ripped to shreds a volume of poetical works from the nineteenth century. Next they set about breaking up sticks of furniture. As they stomped on a mahogany umbrella stand, the sun disappeared behind the clouds and thunder growled in the distance. Angelica prayed the storm would move away from St. Croix, but the minute she put flame to paper, the sky turned pewter and unleashed a carwash load of water onto the woodpile. Rain pellets ricocheted off the pavers. The women got drenched.

"So much for that," Jenn groused, hair dripping wet and her makeup washing off in the downpour.

Angelica towel dried her hair in the master bath, changed clothes, and went upstairs to vent her frustration on a leather punch bag in the gym. In the media room she found Jenn, champagne glass in hand, ensconced in one of the roomy armchairs semi-circled in front of a cinematic screen. A wall displayed shelves of DVDs arranged alphabetically.

"You're just in time for a Bond movie," she told Angelica, jabbing at the remote embedded in the padded armrest.

Angelica pressed Recline on hers, and her seat slid into viewing position. She experimented with the other buttons. From the back of the theater came the rattle of ice collecting in the mini fridge, along with an unmistakable pop-popping sound emanating from the microwave. The densely carpeted floor and windowless walls muted the hiss of the rain to a whisper, and Angelica felt as though she and Jenn were the last two people left in the world, and that they would never be free.

"Here, have some pink bubbly," Jenn said, reaching into an ice bucket.

Discouraged by their dismal attempts at escape, Angelica relaxed in her recliner and tried to lose herself in the movie, although she would have preferred a film without a spy. It reminded her of Dex. Worse, it made her think of the man who had watched them at the office and imprisoned them here.

38

*T*hat night Angelica lay in bed, her mind and heart racing. They had searched each and every room again, systematically. Once the rain abated, they had crossed the courtyard to explore the two symmetrical guest cabanas by the main gate, one decked out in a safari theme, the other done up in French Country, the walls hand-painted in a floral pattern against an exquisite green background. In every part of the property, interior designers had produced breath-taking vistas and areas of intimate comfort. It would have been the perfect home, Angelica reflected as she tried to sleep, if only they were free to leave.

She missed her condo, which she had lovingly decorated on a far smaller scale in cream and blues, and she could not stop worrying about Hercules. Perhaps her downstairs neighbor would hear him yapping from hunger—except that Ed was old and hard of hearing. When she had first moved in, and Herx was still a puppy prone to barking at the slightest provocation, she had considered Ed's deafness a blessing. To make matters worse, nobody had a spare key to her home. She should have given Kathy one, in case of an emergency. But who could have anticipated this?

Later that night, she awoke to male voices outside the French doors. Feeling her way off the bed, she tiptoed to the window and peeked out behind the gossamer drapes to the courtyard. An invasion of Guatemalan gardeners streamed over the bridge, pulling knee-high weeds from the pavers and scaling the rock gardens. As she watched, giant koi chased after them and gobbled them up, teeth zipping through flesh and chomping through bones until there were no humans left. The drapes turned transparent exposing dessert.

Teeth bared and dripping blood, the piranha-koi stared at her with dull fish eyes. She fled back to bed. Scaly heads butted the mullions, splintering wood and shattering glass. They flooded the room attempting to snap at her feet as she wheeled past them on the circular mattress.

"Help, help!" she cried out in terror.

"Angelica, wake up!"

A familiar voice summoned her from the smothering depths, pulling her out of the dark pit of fear. When she opened her eyes, she realized the bed was still and it was her head that was reeling from all the champagne.

Jenn bent over her, prodding her fully awake. "You had a nightmare," she whispered.

"I dreamed the koi were coming to get us."

"Believe me, the koi are the least of our problems. Now go back to sleep."

Angelica did not dare drift back into slumber. Wakeful or asleep, there was no escape.

39

*T*he next morning, Angelica took a slug of mimosa—the hair of the dog. Closing her eyes, she stretched out on the love seat in the den tucked off the master bedroom and looking onto the Japanese garden. Her stomach felt as tight as a coiled spring. She soared through space, higher and higher. When she tried to focus again, the Pierre Bonnard nudes moved on the gold-flecked faux-finish walls. Best not drink *too* much, she cautioned herself through the glorious buzz. Not if they were planning another conflagration in the courtyard once it fully dried out from the rain.

A strip of white linen, which they had attached to a curtain rod, drooped above the front door in the courtyard. They hoped the wind would pick up and someone would see their makeshift flag from the upper story of one of the homes under construction. The flag had been another of Jenn's ideas. She had finished reading *Demise in Paradise* over breakfast and recounted how the heroine tears up her petticoat and ties it to a palm tree growing on the fictional island. A captain in the British Navy spies it through his telescope and orders his frigate into the bay. His crew of sailors find Issy and Lily living in a cave surviving on coconuts, and save them from the marauding pirates.

"Ta-da!" Jenn sang out as rock guitar burst through two slender Bang & Olufsen speakers. "There are thousands of CDs pre-recorded in the thystem," she slurred.

"The Eagles. My dad's favorite band of all time."
Angelica's suppressed her welling tears. Today, she prayed,
their plan would work and they would be free.

Glass in hand, she leaped from the love seat and
pirouetted with forced cheerfulness into the master
bedroom. Peeling her negligee over her head, she went to
investigate the swimwear in the closet. The choice proved
overwhelming, including as it did one-pieces and bikinis—
thong, string, Brazilian, Tanga, boy—all designed for the
curvier woman with size "D" cups.

"Oh, well," she told Jenn. "We can get an all-over tan
while we wait for our bonfire to dry out. It's not as if anyone
can see us."

An assortment of scarves flowed from a rack, one
spangled with the interconnecting "C's" of the Chanel logo,
another a Hermès creation in yellow silk. She grabbed a
handful and flitted through the master bathroom, a rainbow
of color streaming behind her. Stepping into the Japanese
garden, she inhaled the fragrant jasmine from a tree in late
bloom. The star-shaped petals had scattered in the rain and
sprinkled the ground like so much confetti.

A gold scarf tied around her head, Jenn jumped waist deep
into the lagoon, routing the koi into brightly splintering
shards. "It's fr-eezing!" she shrieked, leaping up the wide
rock steps and halting mid-stride on the patio. "Listen! It's
our song!"

A trill of Spanish guitar segued into a slow, seductive
drumbeat. Jenn snatched up Angelica's hand, and the women
began swaying their hips in time to the tempo. At the chorus,
they belted out the refrain, substituting Verona for
California.

"What the heck is going on here?" a man called out from
the house, startling them into sudden paralysis.

Angelica scrambled to cover herself as best she could,

bunching the scarves over her intimate parts. In a half crouch, she looked up and saw Dex standing by the glass shower wall, arms folded. Jenn pulled the bandanna from her hair and concealed her nakedness, though not as fast as she might have done, in Angelica's opinion.

They all stared at each other for a long drawn out moment. Suddenly, Dex sprang into a head-banging routine in time to the refrain, singing at the top of his voice and wildly strumming an imaginary guitar, his blond hair flapping about him.

"How did you know we were here?" Angelica interrupted.

"I didn't. So—you know Maynard?"

"Who? No. We were kidnapped."

Dex took in the idyllic surroundings, a skeptical expression on his face. "You don't look very kidnapped."

"We were, for real," Jenn said.

"Is that limp rag above the front door supposed to be some kind of SOS?"

"How did you get in?" Jenn asked. "Can you get us out? Who is he?" she asked Angelica.

"When you say 'kidnapped,' do you mean you were bundled into a vehicle against your will?"

Angelica shook her head. "Not exactly. But it boils down to the same thing. Can we explain later? He might come back."

"Right. Get dressed while I hotwire the Lamborghini."

"Cool!" Jenn said.

"Mind you," he warned, "it'll be a bit tight even for you skinny girls. I hadn't figured on rescuing any damsels today."

Angelica rebuked Jenn with a look. "Excuse me," she told Dex, "but you can't just go and carjack someone's Lamborghini."

"Sure I can. When I installed the security in the house, I put a vendor's lien on his property. He never paid up. He owes me. Anyway, we have to take his car. I got a ride to St. Croix from my friend at the pro shop. Maynard hasn't settled his account there either."

"You keep talking about this Maynard guy. Who is he?" Angelica demanded.

"Maynard Eric Forbes, founder and CEO of Forbes Biopharmaceuticals, a big outfit in Fort Lauderdale." Dex pulled a wallet from the pocket of his light denim shirt and held up a snapshot. "Recognize this cat?"

Angelica peered at the man in a suit. "Yup, that's Bluebeard."

"Sure is," Jenn said. "How come you keep a photo of him in your wallet?"

Dex grinned wickedly. "I'm in love with the guy. Can't you tell?"

"It's no use, Jenn. You'll never get a straight answer out of Dex."

"Well, what are we waiting for?" Jenn asked. "Dex, how long will it take you to get the car started?"

Angelica glared at her. *"Dex,"* she mimicked to herself. Jenn had certainly changed her tune. Two days before, she was moping around being totally useless, and now here she was trying to run the show to impress him.

"Five minutes," he said. "Ten, tops."

Jenn grabbed Angelica's arm. "C'mon, let's pack." She led the way to the master suite and stuffed a variety of fashion accoutrements into a Louis Vuitton bag.

Once dressed, Angelica made a detour through the kitchen and snatched the jar of plum jelly off the counter and the framed photo of the woman from the library. As they approached the garage, a car engine let out a mighty growl sending tremors through the floor. Dex sat beaming at the wheel of the yellow Diablo.

"What made you so smart?" Jenn asked through the open

window.

Narrowing her eyes at her, Angelica wondered if her colleague had donned the little black chiffon number solely for his benefit.

"MIT," he replied above the engine pulsing at a basso profundo pitch.

"You went to *MIT*?" Angelica asked. There was evidently far more to Dex than met the eye. And he looked pretty hot in the snazzy little sports car, hair tied back for the ride.

The passenger door flipped up, and she ducked inside. As she reached for her seat belt, he turned to help her, and their hands touched, sending sparks through her fingers. At that moment, Jenn's bag landed full force in her lap. Her friend squeezed in beside her.

The garage door clanged into the ceiling. As Dex gunned the car in reverse, Angelica shut her eyes and prayed that nothing would happen to impede their escape.

40

*T*he Lamborghini pivoted in the street and launched out of the Verona enclave and away from their gilded cage.

"How did you get into the house?" Jenn questioned Dex as the car snarled down the road.

"I deactivated the alarm. I got suspicious when I came to find Forbes and couldn't hear the doorbell. I figured he was hiding. The system we installed is palm-activated, but my company has an override."

"How come you installed a two-way alarm so we couldn't get out?" Angelica asked.

"What do you mean?"

"Those flashing red lights on the doors and windows."

"Those contacts alert residents when a kid tries to exit the house. It's a requirement of the Florida Pool Law if there's no fence around the pool."

"What? Oh," Angelica said, feeling extremely foolish. As a real estate agent, she knew about the pool law, but had not figured out what their abductor had done. "He must have switched them out. What would have happened if we'd opened one of the outer doors or windows?"

"An ear-splitting beep would have gone off."

"That's *it?*" Jenn asked. "We wouldn't have been electrocuted?"

Dex glanced at her. "Why would anyone want to electrocute a kid?"

Angelica was reluctant to believe that a harmless device had stood between them and freedom. "Your client Maynard—Eric, or whatever he calls himself—said if we tried to escape, the alarm would notify a guard and they'd be on to us before we could set one foot outside."

Dex shook his head. "He was having you on. You were prisoners of your own device. There was nothing except the burglary alarm and the kid alert system. It was a bluff."

Which we fell for, Angelica thought ruefully, although she was not ready to give in quite yet. "We have reason to believe he murdered Peter Bedford, so we didn't want to take any chances."

"Well, they certainly knew each other," Dex said.

"And you really had no idea we were there?"

He shook his head in wonder. "Sheer fluke. What would you ladies have done if I hadn't showed up?"

"Angelica would have found a way out," Jenn said with heart-warming confidence. "We got close to escaping a couple of times, but Angelica lost her balance in her high heels, and the other time it started to rain."

"Didn't want to get your hair wet, huh?" Dex commiserated, the side of his mouth twitching in amusement.

"It wasn't like that!" Angelica stared daggers at Jenn. "I was literally hanging off the roof by my finger nails, and when we tried to alert someone by resorting to arson, a torrential storm erupted."

"It was more like a hurricane," Jenn added, going one further.

"Really?" Dex asked. "In November? And to think I was ten miles away and missed this phenomenon."

Angelica decided the conversation was going nowhere except making her look a complete idiot, thanks to Jenn's ridiculous comments. So incensed was she, in fact, that it was moments before she realized they had passed the main gate to the community.

"We're free!" she cried as St. Croix receded into the distance.

Dex slid the car into fifth gear. Angelica's stomach turned over in exhilaration, her delight heightened by the proximity of his hip in the cramped space.

"Did you get my email?" she asked.

"I did, Avon Lady."

"Wait. You sell cosmetics door-to-door?"

"No, Jenn." Angelica turned back to Dex. "Why didn't you try and find me?"

"I didn't know you were lost."

"Abducted. Your Maynard Forbes tricked me into going to his house by claiming to be Jenn's father."

"Figures. He's a tricky SOB and a natural born salesman. I bet he was pretty convincing. But I never dreamed he'd resort to imprisonment, perceived or otherwise." He winked at her. "Pretty ingenious plan, if you think about it."

"But why did he do it?"

"I got a feeling we'll find out soon enough."

On the interstate they zoomed past an Oldsmobile with Michigan plates veering slowly between lanes. A wizened man in a hat peered over the rim of the wheel. Angelica and Dex glanced at each other and giggled.

"Shouldn't be allowed," he said.

"My sentiments exactly." Angelica twisted open the lid on the jar of preserve she had brought from the house and dipped in her finger. "This is so good," she moaned, sucking off the sweet plum jelly. "I've never felt so hungry in my entire life."

"Here, give me some of that." Dex caught hold of her wrist and licked her finger. "Mm," he murmured, sliding the whole digit in his mouth while Angelica's nether regions quivered deliciously in response.

"So, do you, like, know each other well?" Jenn asked, watching them with curiosity.

"Well, we've seen each other naked," Dex said, giving Angelica a slow, sexy smile.

"You've seen me naked," Jenn reminded him. "And we don't know one another."

"True," returned Dex. "But you haven't seen me naked."

Jenn opened her mouth.

"Don't even think it!" Angelica warned, cutting her off at the pass with a point of her sticky finger. What had gotten into Jenn all of a sudden? Impossible to reconcile this flirtatious creature with Plain Jane at the office who wouldn't say boo to a mouse.

"Where to now?" Jenn asked, looking innocent.

"I need to get home and feed my dog," Angelica pleaded. "You can call your parents from my place, if you like."

"Shouldn't we go to the police first? After all, we were kept hostage, even if it *was* with kiddie alarms." Jenn laughed gaily, and it was all Angelica could do not to smack her.

"Dog first, police later," Dex said, stopping the car at the gate to the Cascades. "Code?" he asked Angelica.

Of course Dex knew where she lived, just as he seemed to know everything else about her. She reached over his lap and punched in the numbers.

"Gated communities give a false sense of security," he said. "A dog is a better precaution. Smart move there," he told her, which made her feel a bit better after the business of the alarms.

Inserting the spare door key she kept hidden under the flower pot—and choosing to ignore Dex's disbelieving comment as he came up the steps behind her—Angelica called to Hercules. No bark answered, no patter of paws running across the tile to the door. His food and water bowls stood empty in the kitchen. A dash into the laundry room revealed clumps in the litter box. Good boy! But where was he? Anxiously, she set upon a search of the rest of the condo, relieved to find him stretched out on her bed, safe and sound. He grudgingly opened one brown eye.

"We'll let sleeping dogs lie then," she crooned, fondling his ear before leaving him to his nap. "Missed you."

Pointing Jenn in the direction of the house phone, she returned to the kitchen where coffee gurgled in the machine on the counter.

"Dog okay?" Dex asked.

"It's like he never noticed I was gone."

"Maybe he's just sulking."

"Wouldn't put it past him. Mm, great coffee," she said after taking a sip. "Just what I needed."

"Me too. You wouldn't believe the past forty-eight hours." He turned a barstool to face him and sat astride it, elbows propped on the backrest. "I can't remember the last time I shaved, or ate for that matter."

"Want a peanut butter and jelly sandwich?" Angelica offered.

His mouth crinkled into a smile. "A house specialty? Okay, but hold the jelly. I had enough of that."

Angelica swung open the fridge door. "So, what's been going on? You left the restaurant in such a hurry the other day," she said, striving to keep the accusation out of her voice.

"I had to leave for New York. Bella found an email from her husband dated the day before he died. She doesn't check her messages very often, obviously."

"And?"

"Bedford was a major shareholder in Forbes BP and discovered, I guess through Lindy—Maynard's girlfriend— that Maynard had been unloading stock in various marketing deals. That made Bedford suspicious, so he dug around and found out that Forbes was not going to get FDA approval for a newly developed product he'd practically sunk his company into."

Angelica sliced the sandwich in half and handed the plate to Dex. "You're saying Maynard's company was in trouble?"

"That's the understatement of the year. He was millions of dollars in the hole personally. He was embezzling company funds to stay afloat, knowing all the time that Forbes BP was going belly up."

"He owns Divine Canine, right?"

"And Divine Feline, Divine Porcine—"

"Divine Porcine?" Angelica asked.

"Gourmet food for pet potbellied pigs."

"What sort of gourmet food?"

"Truffles."

"That's crazy."

"Totally asinine," Dex agreed. "But it makes a ton of money. Anyway, Forbes was ready to launch a key product called 'Biche,' which replicates female dog hormones in women and is supposed to make them as irresistible to men as a dog in heat is to a prospective mate. The word on Wall Street was that it was going to be as big as those products for erectile dysfunction."

Jenn, who had been listening from the doorway, hoisted herself onto the barstool next to Dex. "Yeah, but you'd think this product would attract any Tom, Dick or Harry."

"More like every Rex, Duke and Rover. Tests showed that dogs reacted more strongly than men, having more acute olfactory senses. So, for every man attracted, there were five dogs in pursuit, all wanting to mate."

"Lends a whole new meaning to the term 'dog lover,' " Angelica remarked. "I think it's a revolting idea."

"Seems like the FDA agreed with you, but it cost Forbes a

billion dollars to have it tested." Dex heaped three sugars into his coffee. "So much for diversifying into products for humans. He should've stuck with fish food."

Jenn whistled. "A billion dollars!"

"He must have bribed a regulator at the FDA for a heads-up, or else it was leaked that the application would get rejected, because on Monday his girlfriend sold thirty-five thousand Forbes BP shares. If Maynard is indicted for insider trading and fraud, he could be looking at a long prison term. But I guess that's the least of his problems." Dex winked at the women. "I wonder what he planned to do with you. Sell you into the white slave trade?"

"Very funny," Angelica said. "So how do you know all this about Forbes?"

"The FDA issued a refuse-to-file letter. Maynard's stockbroker told the cops about Lindy's timely sale of shares and how Maynard tried to dump the rest of his. It's all over the financial news."

Angelica's mind boggled at how much trouble the rich could land themselves in out of sheer greed. Forbes had told her as much on the way to St. Croix. *Physical surroundings have little to do with real happiness.* Perhaps he had seen the light—too late. And to think she had been in the company of that crook!

"None of this explains why you had to go to New York," she told Dex. "Did he murder Peter Bedford?"

"Looks that way. Bella was panicking about the email, thinking Maynard might come after *her*. I forwarded it to the detectives investigating him. I had no idea what a flake he was when I installed that stuff in his house."

Angelica leaned against the breakfast bar. "So your client Bella had nothing to do with her husband's death?"

"Nah, she just wanted a half share of his money if she couldn't have his fidelity. Now she regrets telling Maynard about Bedford's affair with Lindy. Maynard was under a lot of pressure financially. He must've felt like he was losing everything, and Lindy was the last straw. Only, there's no real proof he did commit the murder." Dex pushed back his empty plate. "I got to get going. I called Detective Wright while you were looking for your dog, and he said he'd be over to talk to you."

"Could you drop me off at Plum Realty so I can pick up my rental car?" Jenn asked. "Catch you later," she told Angelica, hugging her at the front door while Dex hung back a short distance.

Then, much to Angelica's delight, he squeezed her close, holding her for a brief instant.

"By the way," he added, pulling a fat wad of bills from his jeans pocket. "From Lindy, with love. Should be more than enough to fix your car."

"Thanks!" Angelica showed him the photo of the blonde. "Is this her?"

"Where did you find that?"

"In Maynard's library. I was going to give it to the police."

Something in Dex's eyes changed, a shutter coming down. "I'll hold on to this, if you don't mind."

"Fine, then," Angelica said, her suspicions confirmed. She had always felt there was something going on between Lindy and Dex, and he had proved it by getting possessive over the photo.

"See ya," he said as he stepped out the front door.

Her recent high spirits in check, Angelica mulled over Dex's relationship with Lindy as she opened a can of dog food. Divine Canine. She would never buy this brand again!

Her thoughts kept returning to Dex. He had said casually he would see her, but when?

41

*H*ercules bounded into the kitchen, skidded on the tile and, recovering his balance, trotted with dignity to his filled bowl. Angelica watched him wolf down his food, glad he had come out of his snit. The poor thing must be starving. She wandered about her condo, happily reacquainting herself with her home, even though it had been only a couple of days since she last saw it. As she entered the dining room, however, she noticed straightaway that something was wrong.

The stacks of papers she had left in neat piles on the table had been rifled. Not only that, but the drawers of her small filing cabinet gaped open. Had Jenn, who had been using the landline phone in the room, poked through her personal files? Angelica felt anger bubble in her throat. Why would Jenn do such a thing? Was she hoping to poach some of her former clients?

Too many strange things were happening to jump to hasty conclusions, she reminded herself. She dialed Jenn's number to leave a message, and found herself speaking to Kim and having to give her an assurance that her roommate was absolutely safe and would, in fact, be home soon, at which time she was to call Angelica. "Immediately," she added. "It's urgent. She just went to pick up her rental car at the office." Fortunately, Jenn had retained the keys on her person when she was taken.

Angelica returned to the kitchen where Hercules had consumed the contents of his bowl and lay curled up on the tile, dosing. "Lazy bones," she teased, rubbing his fleecy belly with her big toe. "I'll take you for a walk later," she promised, but the word "walk" failed to elicit the usual enthusiastic response. Thinking he must be lethargic from hunger, she scooped more food into his bowl.

She poured herself a second mug of coffee, wondering how she would confront Jenn. They had become close at St. Croix, as was normal under the circumstances. Unthinkable that her friend would go behind her back in this way. Upon taking her coffee into the living room, she stopped short. A man's shoe print lay embedded in the carpet, toe pointing toward the lanai. Size eleven, she estimated, crouching over it. Smooth sole. Dex had not been in the living room and, in any case, had been wearing Nike's, which would have left a distinct tread in the vacuumed pile. To her knowledge, nobody but Dex and Jenn had visited her condo since she had cleaned it the weekend she went to the art fair.

She began to panic in earnest when she saw that the slider to the lanai was unlocked, even though she was sure she had checked it the other morning when she left for the office, just as she always did. She called Detective Wright.

"I'm on my way," he said. "Don't touch anything."

She looked through the rest of the condo for signs of unlawful entry. Ten minutes later, hearing a car stutter to a stop outside, she rushed to the window and watched the detective emerge from the driver seat of a dark blue Crown Victoria. She met him at the front door, relieved to see he hadn't brought his partner, Larry Frye.

"Duane Dexter told me about your little vacation at St. Croix Golf & Country Club," Wright joked.

"Five star accommodation," Angelica responded with a rueful smile. "Very exclusive."

She filled him in on the details of the abduction and showed him the shoe print in the living room, which he measured and photographed.

"Any guesses?" he asked.

"I'm assuming it's the man who took us hostage. He had my keys."

"Anything missing?"

"I don't think so. Some boxes have been moved around in the bedroom closet and every drawer was searched, but I don't think it was money or valuables he was after. I mean, he's pretty loaded. Or used to be."

Detective Wright removed his crumpled jacket. "May I?" he asked, indicating a chair at the dining room table.

"Please. Coffee?"

"Thanks, but I already had a lethal dose of caffeine today." He studied the papers on the table. "Forensics will lift prints and look for a match unless, of course, the intruder wore gloves."

Normally, the thought of a forensics team invading her home and leaving print dust all over the place would send her into cardiac arrest, but she knew she would want to clean the condo again in any case now that it had been violated. "Why would he come here?" she asked.

"Did Peter Bedford give you anything for safekeeping?"

"Like what?"

"An envelope. Some—"

"Yes! Yes, he did! He gave me a large sealed envelope. He said it contained documents for his condo."

"Did you read them?"

"No, I never opened the envelope. Shortly after he gave it to me, he died, and what with everything going on, I didn't give it another thought."

"Where is the envelope now?"

Angelica tried to recall what had become of it. "I must

have put it in my briefcase."

Detective Wright shook his head. "Forbes had your briefcase, you said, so why would he come looking here?"

"I don't know. Following Bedford's murder at Plovers Key, a police officer questioned me and took me straight to the station." Angelica winced at the memory. "I never got to my car, so I couldn't have left the envelope there. I could have left it in the police cruiser or at the station."

The detective's mouth turned down at the corners. "It never showed up. Ah, well," he said.

"What was in it? Why is it so important?"

"We're trying to build a case against Forbes. Plus, it would help corroborate someone's testimony."

"Whose?"

"The neighbor in eight-oh-two. When we first questioned him, he said he was in the shower the morning of November fifth and didn't hear a thing. To believe him, he takes hour-long showers. Well, turns out this Ernesto Cruz is an illegal alien. We put the squeeze on him, and he starts singing like a soprano."

"You mean he knows what happened?" Angelica could barely keep still in her chair. "There's a break in the case?"

"Possibly. Cruz was sunbathing in his lounge chair, sipping a Corona," Wright began, referring to a notebook, "when he hears two *gringos* arguing on the balcony to his left. The way he explained it, the voices were loud but controlled."

"Did he understand what they were saying?"

"According to Cruz, the *Americano* was asking where the documents were and accusing the *Inglés* of stealing them from his house. The English guy, whom we can assume to be Bedford, said he gave them to his Realtor."

"Me? Why?"

"Don't yet know the significance of the alleged

documents, but it seems the American wanted them back real bad and threatened Bedford."

"Threatened to kill him?"

"Words to that effect, but it seems Bedford didn't take him seriously enough. According to our witness, there were more heated words, the gist of which concerned a woman. Apparently, the American was accusing Bedford of having also stolen his girlfriend."

Frowning, Detective Wright flipped through his spiral notebook. "No name. Cruz couldn't remember it, but he was adamant it was *la mujer del Americano* that was the subject of the dispute. He says he heard a scuffle, an exchange of blows, and the sound of the balcony rail giving way. Hard to tell if Cruz ascertained this from the newspapers or that's how he actually remembered it."

Wright closed his notebook. "Either way, he couldn't have seen Bedford fall because his condo faces due west and there's that privacy wall. Plus, he's not exactly a credible witness. So those documents he mentioned would be really useful."

"It could have been an accident," Angelica said, frightened to think that a cold-blooded killer might have been in her home and was still at large.

"It's possible the murder was not premeditated," the detective allowed. "The suspect may just have snapped. Even if we get hold of him for questioning, we may never know the truth."

"Do we know where he is?"

"We've reason to believe he followed his girlfriend to California. It's unlikely he'll be back of his own accord. But for your own piece of mind, you may want to change your locks or, better yet, stay with a friend."

Angelica slumped in her chair, fighting back tears of frustration and wishing for her old life back. The thought of snuggling up on her sofa with Hercules, without a real care in the world except who was going to inherit that stupid office at Plum Realty, seemed like heaven at this point.

"My dog must have gone crazy when Forbes walked through the front door," she said. "He's very territorial and protective. In fact, I'm surprised he didn't start yapping when you came in." Or when she brought Dex and Jenn home, for that matter.

"Where is your dog now?" Wright asked.

"Asleep in the kitchen."

"Maybe the intruder threw him a treat and drugged him. After all, Forbes is in the veterinary business."

At this suggestion, a blaze of indignation swept through her. Murder and kidnap were one thing, but drugging a defenseless little dog made her blood boil. "Can we get proof?" she asked.

"You mean test his doo-doo?" Wright wrinkled his nose. "We could check for traces of drugs in his system. Still, if we ever catch up with this guy, breaking and entering and sedation of a pet will be the least of the charges. Well, I think we're done for now." The detective got up. "Anything else, you call me," he said as Angelica escorted him to the front door.

"I do have a question," she ventured. "It's, well, it's about Duane Dexter."

Wright stood patiently before her, jacket bunched over his arm.

"I mean, he seems to know a lot about this case."

"Well, he does have a vested interest in it."

"I guess what I really want to know is if I can trust him," she said in a rush.

Detective Wright flicked her a quizzical look beneath bushy gray eyebrows. "Trust him with your life or your heart, d'you mean?" He stepped across the threshold, paused and shrugged. "I'm a divorced old cop. What do I know? I've solved a number of cases in my time and seen plenty of funny business, but I never did figure out that other stuff. Well, good luck to you anyhow."

"Yeah, thanks," Angelica mumbled after him. So much for that.

The phone started ringing, and she turned back into the condo, hoping against hope it was Dex.

42

*"H*ey, Angelica, it's Jenn," her colleague burbled into her ear on the phone. "I've been telling Kim all about the kidnapping and what we did at the house, all that champagne and skinny-dipping, and stuff. But then I thought, Angelica will be waiting to hear from me so I'd better call."

"I'm glad you did," Angelica said, thankful she didn't have to accuse her friend of prying now. "Listen, Detective Wright just left. I think Forbes broke into my condo while I was away, looking for documents that Bedford supposedly gave me."

"What sort of documents?" Jenn demanded, and Angelica realized she must be worrying about Forbes' whereabouts as well.

"Something bad enough to kidnap us for. But I think I must have misplaced them. Don't worry, though. The detective assured me he'd flown the coop."

"What about Scrob?" Jenn asked.

"What about him?"

"Well, when you said that about the coop, I thought, by association, of chickens, and then of Scrob."

Flighty logic, Angelica thought. "Unless the cop got him on unlawful gun possession, he's probably been released."

"Yeah, because evidently they got the wrong guy. The police must have realized that when his property turned up clean. Well, not clean, because it's actually really filthy, but you know what I mean."

Angelica rubbed her eyes, remembering how exhausting it had been living with Jenn. On the other hand, it was sort of reassuring to have her around after they had shared so much. "Can you stay over at my place tonight?" she asked.

"You okay? You sound weird, kinda hoarse."

"I just want this to be over. I've been thinking about taking a trip to Hawaii and visiting my sister on the way. I gave it a lot of thought while we were at St. Croix. Anyway, we can talk later. Want to order in a pizza?"

"I'll pick one up on the way. I just had a visual of Forbes in his Italian suit showing up at the door delivering pizza on a silver platter."

"You're right. We mustn't open the door to anyone. Pepperoni-mushroom? A bit of a comedown from our recent fare." Angelica gave a wry laugh.

"Angelica? Don't go just yet. Listen. Kim's general manager at the radio station wants us to do an interview! The airtime would get our name out to hundreds of potential clients. We could team up. I've been thinking of slogans. How about: 'Buy and sell with the team from hell'? You know, from us being imprisoned?"

"Did you come up with anything else?" Angelica asked dubiously. "Anyway, you were talking about champagne and skinny-dipping. It makes us sound like we were holed up with Heffner."

"I've got ideas popping out of my head! I need to write them all down. We could say we were starved and had to eat bugs, just for the sympathy angle. Do you think that would sound better?"

"Well, it might get us in as contestants on a reality show."

"You don't sound very enthusiastic," Jenn said in a huff.

"Sorry. I'm just beat."

"Okay. Well, I'll see you later," Jenn said, terminating the call.

Angelica returned to the kitchen to check on Hercules, who lay asleep on the floor. He did seem unusually sleepy, she was thinking when the doorbell drew her to the hallway. Phones, doorbells! So wonderful to hear them again.

"Who's there?" she called through the front door.

"It's Kathy. I brought homemade brownies."

Angelica hugged her friend and invited her in. "How great to see you. I meant to call, but the detective arrived. How are you?"

"Me? I just had root canal. Nothing compared to what you went through. Jenn left a message on my voice mail. I can't believe it! You and Jenn kidnapped! How are you, really, hon? Peter Bedford's murder and now this. And I don't know if you heard, but someone broke into Plum Realty late Wednesday night and set off the alarm. Whoever it was ransacked your cubicle."

"My cubicle?" Angelica cried in outrage. What was so important about these documents that Forbes would risk breaking into her office to look for them?

"Now, don't worry," Kathy said. "I cleaned everything up—I know how you are. But Broker Bob totally lost it. He's feeling very fragile after everything that's happened. He's on meds."

"I'm the one who should be on meds," Angelica retorted.

She poured coffee into two mugs and took them to the breakfast nook.

"Paula at the title agency told me she had noticed a man in a Merc casing our building," Kathy said. "She thought it was strange, but at the time assumed he was a married suit secretly dating one of our agents."

"That could've been Forbes waiting for an opportunity to lure me to his luxurious prison."

"Let's hope he doesn't come back for you."

"You don't think he will, do you?" Kathy could be uncannily right about things. "Is that what you *feel* is going to happen, or were you simply throwing it out as a remote possibility?" Angelica interrogated.

"Oh, hon, don't get your pantyhose in a twist." The office manager tentatively touched her jaw. "I don't know what I'm saying. I'm still on pain medication."

"Kathy! I need you to be lucid. There's a corporate killer on the loose who harbors a freaky obsession for a manila envelope. He may have returned to St. Croix to torture its whereabouts out of me."

What he would do when he found his captives gone, along with the Lamborghini and most of his vintage champagne, was anybody's guess.

43

*T*he next afternoon, Angelica picked up her car from Plum Realty, on the way home purchasing a supply of sponges to finish the clean-up of her condo, which a team of technicians had gone through with a fine-toothed comb. A sample of Hercules' bodily fluids, taken under growling protest, had been sent to the lab. The best way to keep calm, she had discovered, was to keep busy. And try not to worry about Forbes.

She parked in her garage and walked around the car to the passenger side to retrieve the groceries. The duct tape was peeling off at the corners, reminding her about her appointment at the body shop. In the meantime, she looked about for the roll of tape to replace the old piece, realizing after a thorough search that the roll had disappeared. So too the shears she had used to cut the tape and which she had propped against the far wall.

Arms laden with bags, she slammed the car door closed with her hip, wondering what could have happened to those two items. As she turned, a figure backlit by the sun stepped into the garage, shears raised. Her bags fell to the floor. She glanced frantically about her. She had not left enough room to get around the hood of her vehicle. The man approached, and she screamed.

"Angelica? You all right? It's me, Ed Thomas, your neighbor."

"Oh, Ed." She gasped in relief. "I thought you were someone else."

"Sorry to scare you. Here, let me help with those." Sending his paper airplane sailing into the air, he bent arthritically for the groceries.

"I thought you were holding a pair of shears."

"No, no, just my plane. I saw you drive in and wanted to say hello. You were gone a few days."

"You didn't happen to notice a distinguished-looking man in a Rolls while I was away, did you?" Angelica asked, realizing that nosy neighbors sometimes had their uses.

"Can't say that I did. Sorry. I'll keep a better look out for you in future. It's not like you have many gentlemen visitors, though I can't for the life of me understand why," Ed said kindly.

"It's not like that! The man's dangerous. He's medium build, in his fifties. If you see someone fitting his description lurking around here in a luxury vehicle, you need to call the police."

"Will do," Ed said, taking the groceries to the foot of the steps.

She made a mental note to contact Detective Wright and let him know that something went missing after all. Perhaps Forbes was planning a second abduction. Or had she simply misplaced the duct tape and sheers? She retrieved Ed's origami airplane from the grass and returned it to him before hurrying up the steps to her condo.

The sooner she left town, the better. Fortunately, she was able to reserve a flight to Honolulu at short notice and lost no time packing. Her dad had insisted on paying for her ticket. The prospect of visiting him made her weep tears of joy. Nor could she wait to see her sister, who had promised to deliver her top-secret news when Angelica stopped over in L.A.

Sorting through the hangers in her closet, she selected items to drop off at the dry cleaner's prior to her trip. She paused when she came to the gray suit she had worn for the meeting with the Epsteins. How could she ever wear this suit again and not remember that dreadful day? Emptying the jacket pockets, she pulled out a couple of her business cards. What was it about these cards and that suit? She chased the elusive memory around the corners of her mind until her eyes fell on a bikini folded next to the suitcase on the bed. Of course!

She leaped for the phone and speed-dialed Detective Wright's number. "I just remembered," she told him breathlessly. "I left the envelope in the poolside restroom at Plovers Key after I left Peter Bedford. I never put it in my briefcase. I was washing my hands, and a woman in a bathing suit started talking to me about real estate. I gave her one of my cards. I guess I just forgot all about the documents."

"Okay, Miss Lane, I'll check it out. Hopefully someone turned it into the front desk."

"I'm not usually so careless."

Detective Wright clucked away her apology. "I'll let you know," he said, ending the call.

In spite of his assurances, Angelica reproached herself for having possibly delayed progress in the case. She had two days until she left for Hawaii and would not feel safe until Forbes was in custody.

44

Angelica bundled Hercules into the backseat of her Camry on an unseasonably hot and muggy morning that made her sunglasses steam up when she got into the car. When she arrived at Plum Realty, she left the air running for the dog's benefit while she went to tie up some loose ends before leaving on vacation. Kathy had offered to look after Hercules at her house, which had a fenced-in back yard.

How wonderful it would be to relax far away from it all. Away from Plum Realty. Away from the snowbirds. Away from the police investigation and from Forbes, assuming he was still in town. Away from Dex.

That, she admitted to herself, might be hard.

In the rear window, Hercules jumped up and down, mimicking a wind-up toy, his yelps echoing across the parking lot. She had better be quick before someone complained. Unfortunately, her first order of business involved a private meeting with Broker Bob. She would use the excuse of the air left on in her car to get away sooner.

Blah-blah-blah, she thought ten minutes later, fixing him with a fake smile while he droned on about the dream home at the St. Croix Golf & Country Club.

"Yes, I remember the Verona," he reminisced from behind his desk, leaning back in his burgundy leather chair. "It won a Prestigious Properties award, quite justifiably in my opinion."

Conscious of having left Hercules in the car for a while now, Angelica waited on the edge of her seat for her boss to dismiss her.

"It has an extensive aquatic facility, does it not?" Broker Bob inquired.

"A large pool, yes," she said, shifting in her chair. "And koi pods." Detective Wright had promised to see to the fish.

"And I'll never forget the utopian sanctuary accessible via disappearing sliders."

"You must mean the Japanese garden."

"And that *trompe l'oeil* in the dining room!"

"You got me. Is that something edible?" And then she remembered: Broker Bob must be referring to the mural that gave the illusion of a view of a Tuscan landscape through a painted arched doorway.

"Un-believable!" he exclaimed.

Broker Bob had trouble believing anything, it seemed. Angelica decided he had probably exploded the myth of Santa Claus and the tooth fairy before he ever had a tooth. It was, come to think of it, impossible to imagine him without spectacles and a red bowtie even as a babe in his crib. He pounded his fist on the desk, and she jumped.

"How do you do it?" he cried. "How do you manage to get so many people in trouble? Maynard Forbes, for goodness sake! His house is worth millions!"

"Technically it's not his house to dispose of since the Feds are freezing his assets," Angelica said.

"The FBI wouldn't be involved if you hadn't interfered. Nor would the SEC, or the CIA, for all I know."

"That's B.S. They were already onto him."

Broker Bob gripped the desk. "What good is Forbes to us in prison?"

"He could keep Scrob company," Angelica joked, far beyond caring. After all, it wasn't Broker Bob who had come to within an inch of his life.

"If they ever catch up with his private jet, Maynard Forbes will be vacationing in Club Fed. He won't be in lockdown with the likes of Russell Scrob."

Angelica briefly indulged in a vision of Scrob in a Day-Glo orange jumpsuit. "Don't forget two counts of kidnapping," she pointed out. "Abduction is not a white-collar crime."

Broker Bob looked regretful, as though he rather wished she had never resurfaced at all. "And not content with getting yourself mixed up in all this, you had to drag another associate down with you."

"That was a case of mistaken identity," Angelica protested. "Jenn rented a car like mine."

"But you had to go over to Mr. Scrob's residence, against my express advice not to, I might add. Your meddling landed him in jail and lost us yet another listing. He may sue Plum Realty. He's just the type."

"I'm sorry you see it that way. I just wanted to help Jenn."

"Ms. Lane," Broker Bob spluttered. "Do us all a favor and do not help anymore. Just make sure you take that vacation. In this one instance," he implored in staccato, "please do as you are told."

Angelica sprang from her chair. "Fine. I'm going!"

She flounced out of his office, feeling light as air now that her vacation was truly about to begin. She picked up a couple of items from her cubicle and went out to the car to get Hercules.

"Come to Mommy," she cooed, picking him up. "You're going to stay with Aunt Kathy. Yes, you are! You'll like that, won't you? Yes, you will!"

She tickled his ears but, sensing that something was up, he sprang out of her arms the moment they reached reception. As she bent to catch him, he shot away, dragging his leash.

Grooff, grooff, grooff!

"Hercules! Stop that this second!" she hissed. If Broker Bob heard him, she was doomed.

Grooff, grooff, grrr-ooff!

"This must be Mighty Mutt," Rick exclaimed, stepping out of the conference room just in time for Hercules to clamp the agent's well-pressed pants in his teeth.

"Sorry," Angelica said. "He doesn't like men much."

"No shit! Get him off of me, can't you? This is my good Armani suit, for crissakes!"

Kathy ventured from behind the reception desk, holding out a Saltine. "Here, boy," she coaxed.

As Rick tried to shake himself loose, Angelica hopped from one foot to the other, attempting to cajole her pet into some semblance of obedience. The growling turned into a howl. Agents crowded around the desk, watching Rick fling his leg and Hercules cling to it with equal determination, everyone cheering the dog on and exclaiming enthusiastically. Finally, Rick kicked so hard that the little dog flew through the air taking a wad of expensive fabric with him, eliciting a collective groan of sympathy from the audience when he landed with a thump on the carpet.

"You hurt him!" Angelica cried even as her pet returned to the fray.

Rick raised his fists, his face a bilious crimson. "Keep this little runt off me, goddammit!"

A middle-aged couple walked through the main door, the bell barely audible above the ruckus of phones, growls and curses, only to turn around and head back out to the parking lot, expressions of shock on their faces. Hercules made contact with Rick's other pant leg, black marble eyes glinting up at his rival.

"Take off your pants," Kathy suggested. "I can't answer the phone with all this commotion going on. People will think they've reached Animal Abuse Central."

"He's abusing *me*!" Rick snarled, limping toward the conference room, dog attached to his ankle. Edging behind a chair, he unfastened his belt.

Angelica flew to the doorway. "Don't whip him!"

"Only if he bites me." Rick unzipped and bent down to remove his shoes and pants, gingerly shaking out his ambushed leg.

As he straightened up, Hercules leaped away, jerking the garment from his hands. He tore past Angelica, dragging the pants along the carpet. By this time, everyone except Rick and Angelica were hooting with laughter. The dog bolted into the sales area.

"Hercules, bad, very bad!" Angelica shouted, pouncing on him.

Broker Bob stormed out of his office and took in the sales staff loitering by the front desk, Rick in his plaid boxers, and Angelica clutching the dog and a torn pair of man's pants. "A moment more of your time, Ms. Lane," he said stonily, holding his door open for her. "And do not even think about bringing that fiend in here with you."

Angelica bundled the dog over to Kathy and steeled herself for the final confrontation.

45

"**M**s. Lane," Broker Bob began, spraying spittle. "You are, frankly, an embarrassment and a distraction to this office. Scandal courts you! Disaster stalks you!"

He mopped his livid brow with a red silk handkerchief. "Turn the air up!" he yelled across the desk to Phil passing outside the door, as the phrase "apoplectic fit" floated on an biplane banner through Angelica's brain.

Settling back in his chair, Broker Bob took a measured breath. "When you started, I had high hopes for you. And you have done, uh, tolerably well. Until now."

Stung by the injustice of his statement, Angelica had to force herself to remain composed in her chair.

"We agreed upon a brief leave of absence while all the unpleasantness surrounding the Bedford case dies down, but I really think we would all prefer it if you decided to hang your license elsewhere. I still can't see how you let so many listings slip through your fingers. And now you have the temerity to bring a dog to work. It *is* your dog?"

"Yes."

"Of course it is."

"Kathy's looking after him while I'm away," Angelica explained. "I was going to cover the front desk for five minutes while she took him home, but he escaped."

"Escaped! And what stunt can we expect from you next time?" Sneering, Broker Bob rubbed thumb against fingertips in ominous fashion. "More explosions, murder, and general mayhem?"

Angelica leaned forward in her chair. "Who knows?" she said with a malicious smile. As if she was responsible for everything that had happened! "Now, if you'll excuse me, I have a plane to catch."

Jumping up, she bid Broker Bob good day. Maybe she *should* go and work elsewhere, she thought in a surge of indignant rage. However, Plum Realty was close to home and Kathy was the best office manager anyone could wish for. She had gotten used to the place and the people—even Broker Bob, who, it must be said to his credit, maintained a good reputation with the home-owning public.

She made her way toward reception where Hercules sat tethered to a file cabinet, head tilted to one side as he watched his mistress approach, a worried look in his eyes. Her heart dipped at the prospect of leaving him, especially when he might think it was because he had been naughty. Which, of course, he had been.

Kathy was still chuckling at his antics. "Tyler got it all on his phone. He's going to post a 'Rabid Dog Attacks Realtor' video on YouTube." She removed her glasses and wiped the tears from her eyes. "Now, don't worry, hon. You know I'll take the best care of Herx. Just relax and enjoy your trip."

"Sorry my time got taken up by Broker Bob, and you couldn't take Herx home. But I'm sure he'll behave himself now."

"Phil and I are going to take him now. Jenn's covering the desk. But you owe Rick a new suit."

After making a fuss of the dog and promising Kathy a souvenir from Hawaii, Angelica got in her car and drove south on 75 to the toll, checking the needle on the gauge to make sure she had enough gas to get across the Alley. The long stretch of highway through the Everglades offered no services other than periodic restrooms with snack machines, and scenic stops with boat ramps overlooking alligator-infested water. Somewhere around here, Rusty Scrob's brother had met his end under suspicious circumstances. Best not to dwell on that, she decided.

No sooner had she assured herself she had enough fuel to take her to Miami Airport than she heard a strange sound coming from the trunk. At least it wasn't the engine. The intermittent thumping disconcerted her nonetheless. A car part coming loose? Then, just as suddenly as the noise started, it ceased. Perhaps her suitcase had shifted position in the trunk. That must be it. No need to panic, she told herself. It couldn't possibly be something else going wrong.

46

Angelica reached airport parking without further mishap and found a space close to the shuttle stop, where a handful of passengers gathered with their baggage. She began, finally, to get in the vacation mood, looking forward to her long-postponed trip to Hawaii.

She grabbed her bag from the passenger seat and got out of her Camry. Rounding the car, she sprang open the trunk with her remote. "Aaarrh!" she cried, stumbling backward in panic when she saw the snake coiled around her suitcase.

"Yo! Whazzup?" asked a young passerby in low-riding shorts. "Holy sh**!" he exclaimed, peering out at a safe distance from beneath his back-to-front cap.

A second man—tanned, mid-thirties—approached, wielding a titanium golf club. "Is it an anaconda?" he asked, eyeballing the scaly, black-on-brown patterned body.

The youth shrugged into a crotch-grabbing move and started to rap:
"She got a anaconda-ah,
In the trunk of her Honda-ah . . ."

"It's a Toyota," Angelica corrected. "And the make of snake is python. I suspect my ex-client put it there." At this point, she lost all composure. "I have to get my suitcase out of the trunk right now! I'm already late. I don't want to miss my flight!"

"Are pythons venomous?" Golf Pro inquired.

"They jus' squeeze you to death, bro," Hip-Hop informed him.

Angelica used her new cell phone to call Wright at the police station, informing him that if this was Scrob's snake, the owner would have to come to the airport to claim it, and warning the detective she had better not find a ferret in her suitcase. Furthermore, she wanted to know if planting a snake in someone's car carried a moving traffic violation, reflecting that nothing would give her greater pleasure than to see Scrob marched straight back to jail.

"He is out on probation," Wright confirmed, and suggested that aggravated assault and burglary might be appropriate charges for illegally entering a person's car for the purpose of introducing a dangerous reptile.

Golf Pro flagged down the shuttle with his club. The driver got down from the bus and shambled over to Angelica's car.

"That's a big'n!" he observed, gawking in dismay at the snake in the trunk.

Angelica let rip a sigh of exasperation. "It's not mine! It's a stowaway. What am I going to *do*?" She was determined to catch her flight, and she'd be darned if some weasely little redneck and his forked-tongued accomplice were going to stop her.

"I'll radio it in to Port Authority," the driver said, clambering back up behind the wheel.

The bus rumbled forward to the stop, where a red-faced woman stood yelling at Golf Pro and pointing to her watch.

"We have a flight leaving for L.A.," he explained to Angelica. "If we don't get going, they won't let us check in our bags."

"I'm flying to L.A. and then on to Honolulu. That suitcase contains gifts for my family and all my clothes. I can't leave without it!"

"No sweat," he said, cautiously prodding the snake with his golf iron.

"Its tail is flickin' you off, man," Hip-Hop warned.

The reptile wound its neck around the pole as the rest of its body slithered in a giant Slinky over the edge of the trunk. Golf Pro, perspiring through his sport shirt, finally managed to wriggle his club free, and the snake writhed away in a long series of *S's* across the asphalt and disappeared beneath a parked minivan. Thanking the golfer, Angelica dove for her suitcase on castors and, locking the car, bolted after the bus.

At the terminal building, she checked in her luggage and waited to pass through security control, arriving breathlessly at the gate just as her row was being called. Jostling her carry-on through the first class aisle to coach, she scanned the cabins. Even now, she could not be sure she had left her life behind. After all, a snake had followed her across state. She was, undeniably, a woman with enemies.

Propelled forward by the long line of people boarding, she located her window seat beside a Japanese businessman, and hefted her bag into the overhead bin. Over the headrests, she scrutinized the influx of passengers.

"Give Wendel two scoops," a housewifely passenger seated across the aisle instructed someone on her cell phone. "And make sure it's Divine Canine Treats. But only if he's been really-really good," she rabbited on to Angelica's irritation.

Why did the woman have to mention Divine Canine of all things? Fortunately, the captain came on the P.A. system at that moment and drowned out her flow of words. Any turbulence would be mild, he assured his passengers in a soothing transatlantic accent, and every indication pointed to a calm and pleasant flight. As long as he didn't attempt to put the aircraft into reverse, Angelica thought with a shudder. Succumbing to his soporific bedside manner, she nodded off for a while, awakening to the motion of the plane taxiing down the runway.

She opened the magazine she had saved for the six-hour flight. A cover line had caught her eye on the kiosk rack: *"Thirteen Reasons He Hasn't Called."*

Wondering about Dex's failure in this regard, she flipped through the glossy pages. She had left him a message saying she was going to Kauai, hoping he would call to wish her a safe trip. The article, featured under "Straight Talk," a section written by men for women who wanted to demystify the male species, read, "You wait in nail-biting suspense for that call. *The Call* that will decide the future of your love life. He's stylish, smart, and has that indefinable quality that makes you just *know* he's Mr. Right. So why doesn't he call?"

Why indeed? Riveted, Angelica read the thirteen possible reasons:

"1) He doesn't want to.
2) He wants to, but can't work up the nerve.
3) He decides to play it cool and wait a day or so.
4) He can't think of anything to say.
5) He's waiting for tix to the game to impress you.
6) He was run over by a bus.
7) He lost your number.
8) He ran out of cellular minutes.
9) He prefers blondes.
10) He prefers brunettes.
11) He's trying to score with someone else first.
12) He's gay.
13) He forgot."

Was there ever a good reason why a man doesn't call? she wondered. Reason number nine gave her pause, even though Dex had said he preferred brunettes. He could be with Lindy

Weiss right now; he could have taken her to Dragonfly Island! Besides, he owed her dinner! He had promised.

Perhaps something terrible had happened.

Relax, she told herself.

A flight attendant served her a soft drink, and Angelica settled back to enjoy the spectacle of the sun fading behind pink-tinged clouds beyond the small window. It was time to put the past behind her. She focused instead on the prospect of seeing her sister in L.A., where she had a four-hour layover. There was never a dull moment with Claire, whose secret would finally be divulged—whatever it was. With her, time seemed to exist in another dimension.

47

"Where are you?" Angelica yelled into her phone as she dodged her way along the busy concourse past throngs of weary passengers laden with baggage.

"Approaching the airport." Claire sounded breathless, as usual. "Wait by the taxi ramp and be ready to jump in."

Lungs filling with fumes, Angelica sat on her suitcase, watching the cars and cabs pull up in front of the LAX terminal building. The moment a peppermint green Renault screeched to a stop at the curb, she hopped off her perch.

"Jelly!" cried a slight figure in skintight jeans, scooting around the car and hugging her close.

Angelica felt gawky beside her younger sister, who had the lithe grace of a dancer. As Claire threw the bags in the trunk, her sequined tank top rode up, revealing a winged tattoo at the base of her spine. Angelica collapsed in the passenger seat, glad to be rid of the airport for a few hours.

Before she could attach her belt, the car lurched forward, flinging her over the dashboard. "What's the rush?" she demanded, bracing her hands just in time.

"Sorry! It's *so* good to see you," Claire squealed. "How was your flight from Miami?"

"Long," she answered, suppressing a yawn. "But I'll sleep on the leg to Honolulu."

"Then a short hop to Kauai and you'll be with Dad."

"Can't wait," Angelica said in tender anticipation. It had

been too long since she'd last seen her father. "Where are we going for dinner?"

"The Thai Orchid Café on Sunset. You in the mood for Thai food?"

"Am I finally going to meet Sam?"

"The band has a gig tonight. We could go see them, but it won't give us much time."

Angelica shook her head against the seatback as the car gathered momentum on the freeway. "That's okay. I'd rather talk. I'm bursting to know what you wanted to tell me in your note."

"Later. First, I want to hear about your adventures. You should write a book. Perhaps we could sell it to Hollywood. I could play Jenn from the office."

Claire had taken acting classes over the past few years and gone for a couple of auditions.

"You could," Angelica conceded. "But you'd have to grow out your hair."

"This is so exciting. Were you in love with him?"

"Who?"

"Bedford! The murdered client you were telling me about. I must say, a married man is a huge step for you."

"No, I was not in love with him. Although he did have a very magnetic personality. You know, I still can't believe he's dead."

Or that she had escaped, for that matter.

*****

He watched Angelica hop into the wacko-woman's jalopy outside the terminal building. The car sped away as though someone were on their tail. Little did she know . . .

48

*B*y the time Angelica finished telling Claire in detail about her days spent confined at St. Croix with Jenn and how they had made their escape, the sisters were driving down an L.A. street past aging blocks of storefronts lit with tawdry Christmas decorations.

"It's still hard to imagine all that stuff happening to you," Claire remarked.

"It was a case of being in the wrong place at the wrong time. Knowing that a confrontation with Forbes was inevitable, Bedford must have decided to give me the documents for safe-keeping to retrieve when he saw me the next day. Only, he never lived to see the next day. With Bedford dead, Forbes' secret, whatever it was, would have been safe."

"Except that you had the envelope."

"Right. Even if he hadn't seen me leave the condo, he would have found out that I was Bedford's Realtor from reading the newspapers. Bedford had told him he'd given me the documents. But Forbes got me and Jenn mixed up and had to wait for another opportunity to kidnap me so he could look through my briefcase and get the keys to my condo and office."

"But you left the envelope in the ladies' room."

"Unluckily for him."

Angelica found it an immense relief to be able to tell her sister the whole story with the objectivity that comes from distancing oneself in time and place. Now, perhaps, she could put everything into perspective, including her feelings for Dex.

"Oh, I just love this Adele song," Claire exclaimed, adjusting the volume on the radio. She began to seat-dance, head bobbing to the soulful lyrics—and almost ran down a pedestrian. "My bad," she mouthed to the man. Seeing her apologetic face, he simply smiled. Her sister had always been able to get away with murder.

When they skidded to a stop minutes later, the sudden stillness of the car seemed unreal. Angelica uncurled her toes and unfastened her seat belt. They were parked on a wide boulevard lined with restaurants and boutiques. Tucked in the surrounding hills, mansions dispatched sleek cars through gated driveways. A pleasant change from the flat topography of Florida.

Claire opened the passenger door and all but yanked her out of the seat. "C'mon, I'm starving," she said, and marched her down the sidewalk and into a café featuring bare tables and bamboo wall hangings. "It's not very ambient but the food's good and cheap."

"We'll go Dutch," Angelica insisted, following her sister to a booth.

"No, Jelly, I'm paying. Contrary to appearances, I can afford it. But we'll have to split dessert."

Angelica slid along the leatherette bench and shrugged out of her light wool jacket. "Makeup artist to the stars!" she said, smiling fondly at her younger sister.

"Cosmetologist, *please.*"

An Oriental girl in Western clothes handed them menus. Claire ordered a Singha beer and the green vegetable curry with jasmine rice.

"Wery good," the server said. "For both?"

Angelica nodded. "But I'll have a hot tea."

"And one fried ice cream to follow," Claire added. "To share."

"Wanilla or chocolate?"

"Chocolate!" Claire and Angelica chimed in unison, and then laughed at each other.

Claire rested her heart-shaped face in her palms. A nose stud accentuated her flawless skin. Disdaining her natural beauty, she wore her hair cropped and gelled into puce-tipped cones. Angelica reflected what a mismatched pair they must present to the diners at the restaurant, although closer study revealed a highly diverse demographic and a few customers of indeterminate gender.

"So, this Dex dude you mentioned," Claire began with a mischievous twitch of the mouth.

"Well, like I said, he rescued me and Jenn. He was our knight in shining armor."

Claire waited with an expectant look.

"But he's not really my type," Angelica concluded.

"Does your type even exist?" her sister demanded. "I mean, it's like you never got over your Ken doll. *Mom's* Ken doll. If you ask me, you're still looking for Mr. Conventional in a red sports car."

"That's not true! Dex has long hair and a tattoo, and rides a Harley!"

Claire's lips curled up in a grin, imprinting deep dimples in her cheeks. "Interesting."

Angelica did not tell her sister that Dex had arrived at the Italian restaurant with his abundant blond hair tied back in a ponytail, and wearing a white shirt and tie. In short, a complete transformation from the biker at the art fair.

"Earth to Jelly," Claire interrupted her reverie.

The server brought their drinks. Angelica squeezed a slice of lemon in her cup.

"You're blushing!" Claire teased.

"Not! It's the steam from the tea."

Claire shook her head in pity. "Jelly, you are *so* confused over this dude. Where did you say you met him?"

Sighing at her sister's persistence, Angelica explained about the painting she had been thinking of buying for her condo when she caught Dex spying on her. "The scene reminded me of our family vacation in Italy. Do you remember?" she asked.

"Yeah, I do," Claire said with a misty look in her eyes. "Gonna send him a 'Wish You Were Here' postcard from Hawaii?"

"Think what you like." Angelica eyed her pretty sister. "Now, then. What does Sam look like? Probably as drop-dead gorgeous as his predecessors, huh?"

"How d'you imagine the lead singer of the Cherry Pops to look like? It's an all-girl rock band, for goodness' sake." Claire's shimmery pink mouth spread into an impish smile.

"Sorry, I'm a bit jetlagged. I know you're trying to tell me something." Angelica rubbed her forehead. "You mean . . ."

"I'm gay. That's what I wanted to tell you."

Angelica's hand trembled as she lifted her cup. She set it back down on the saucer. Claire had always been full of surprises, but this took the biggest prize ever.

"Samantha and me—"

"No way!"

Claire sat back in her seat. "*That's* why I decided not to tell you on the phone. I knew you'd react like this."

Angelica leaned across the table. "How do you know for sure? It could be just a phase. I know women who are bi. Well, not personally, but I have friends who have friends who are bi." She picked up her cup again. "Mom's going to kill you."

"Yeah, well, I'm gonna wait until you're married before I tell her."

"Don't hold your breath. Did you tell Dad?"

"He's totally cool with it," Claire said airily. She began to say something else, but clearly thought better of it. "And I am not bisexual. That's for earthworms."

The server arrived with their curry, and Claire ordered another beer.

Angelica raised an eyebrow. "Don't forget you're driving me back to the airport."

"You sound just like Mom. I know," Claire said, flipping her palm. "Forget I said anything."

Their mother, however, was a safe and familiar topic, and they fell to discussing their stepdad, boring-but-nice Dave, who owned a chain of electronics stores in Portland. He had given Angelica a stud-finder the previous Christmas. She wasn't sure how it worked, but the name sounded promising. When Dave explained it was for locating two by four's in the wall to hang pictures, she was severely deflated. She and Claire debated what they might find in their stockings this year. After moving on to the subject of their father's new love interest, Angelica began to feel drained. She couldn't keep up with all the changes in her life.

Claire glanced at her with concern. "You're not eating. I shouldn't have told you about me and Sam."

"I'm fine with it. Really. I just didn't see it coming, that's all." Angelica let out a heavy sigh. "You and Dad are so far away. Sometimes I wish I could go back to the way things were before our parents split up. And before I met Peter Bedford. Life was more predictable then."

"You're just evolving as a person, Jelly, and that's always scary. You were so in control of your life before that you never let it happen. It took this guy's murder to kick you out of your groove."

Dex had said something about her being stuck in a groove. Angelica realized with a sweet pang in the stomach that she missed him more than she cared to admit. Oh, why hadn't he called?

49

*T*he next morning Angelica deplaned at Lihue after a night at a Honolulu motel. She made for the terminal exit. On the other side of the glass, a lanky figure in jeans and aviator sunglasses waved his arms in her direction.

"Dad!" she yelled, hurtling her baggage cart through a crowd of people dressed in aloha shirts and muumuus bloating in the breeze.

He clasped her in a tight embrace. "Welcome back to Kauai!"

"Dad, you look great!"

It was true, even though the brown hair post-maturely graying at the temples of his lean and tanned face needed a trim, and his plaid cotton shirt was beginning to fray at the collar. He led her to his Jeep and stowed the luggage in the back. Once they were seated, he nodded at a laminated photo dangling from the rearview mirror, where a Hula doll had previously been suspended. "That's Nuala."

The woman with dark tresses pinned up from her face smiled into the camera, her cheek resting against her father's.

"She looks lovely. I'm so happy for you, Dad. And it's great to be here!"

"I'm relieved to see you, Princess. I've been worried to death. Did they catch the guy?"

"Not yet."

"If I'd known, I'd have flown to Florida in a heartbeat.

I'm glad that private investigator found you both safe."

"I know you would have come, Dad. But I'd just as soon forget about it for now."

As Angelica gazed out at the bright hibiscus and fiery bird of paradise aligning the airport road, she felt light years away from mainland USA. Scores of roosters pecked at the rust-colored soil along the highway. To the north, lush green hills rose into a central mountainous region, gray in the distance and culminating in a peak enshrouded by perpetual cloud.

"I have some wonderful news," her dad said, breaking the silence. "Nuala's expecting."

Angelica found she could not speak. And yet she should be used to shocks and surprises by now. She was going to have a half-sibling?

"A boy," her father said, as though reading her thoughts. "We had an amnio done because Nuala's in her early forties. But everything checked out just great."

Angelica privately hesitated about the wonderfulness of the news. After all, her dad was fifty-four. Did Claire know about the baby and been keeping his secret so he could tell his eldest daughter himself? Claire, as she'd been discovering, was good at keeping secrets, although there had been that moment at the restaurant when she looked as though she might be about to say something.

"How about a drink to cool off?" her father suggested as they exited the tunnel of eucalyptus trees leading to Koloa. He pulled into a strip mall behind a Polynesian Adventure Tours bus disgorging tourists adorned with leis, and led Angelica through an ice cream parlor and upstairs to a bar, where they ordered their beverages.

"How's Hercules?" he asked, removing his sunglasses and selecting a table opposite a male duo plucking slack key guitars.

"He's an unholy terror, Dad."

"Your mother did say that getting you a puppy when you were moving into a new condo was a bad idea," he said with a wink. The gloom of the bar accentuated the blue of his eyes and softened the lines on his face.

"Mom thinks everything is a bad idea except marrying a rich man, bless her."

"No hope for your sister then." Her dad chortled. "Poor Claire. I'd love to be there when that goes down."

A buff youth brought a beer and a Mai Tai garnished with a cherry and a pineapple wedge.

"*Mahalo*," Angelica thanked him. She sipped through the straw at the rum, Curaçao liqueur, and lime juice cocktail.

"Right on," the server drawled, teeth blinding white in his mocha-brown face, the long black ringlets reminding her of Dex's blond ones. She never ceased to be amazed at how happy and friendly the people were on the islands.

Limbs sprawling from the chair, her father shook loose a cigarette from the packet. "D'you mind?"

She shrugged. After all, a window stood open behind him. Her mother, however, had never been able to abide his smoking. "I often wonder how you and Mom ever got together," she remarked.

"She fell pregnant with you. We married, and then Claire came along. We stuck it out as long as we could."

Angelica stared at him. "I was conceived out of wedlock?"

"C'mon now, Princess. There's no shame in it. We were in love."

"But Mom said I was premature."

"Well, in a sense you were."

"She might have told me!"

"In Susan's case, it was probably hard to admit she made a mistake. Not that you were a mistake," he said, squeezing Angelica's hand across the table. "Not at all. I'm proud of my two girls."

"That explains why she always made me feel like I was never good enough." Tears pricked her eyes. "I tried so hard to be perfect!"

Her father waved his cigarette in an arc. "Just be yourself, Princess. You *are* perfect. So—how about a ride in the whirlybird before we go home?"

Home for her dad was a comfortable white clapboard bungalow featuring a double pitch tile roof in the Hawaiian style and a wide wooden porch spanning the rear. The house was at complete variance with the imposing structure that had gone up in Portland, and which her mother had decked out in the finest selections from top home furnishing stores.

"Nothing like taking to the air to get away from it all," her dad said.

As he fished in his jeans pocket for cash, the opening bars of "Hotel California" floated across the bar from a pair of mammoth-size speakers, giving her a gut-wrenching turn. She could not shake the premonition that her past had come back to haunt her. The song played insistently in her head all the way to the airfield.

"It's this one," her dad announced upon re-emerging from the trailer office of Trans-Island Helicopters and pointing to a red chopper waiting on its pad on the other side of a chain-link fence.

As the rotor blades started whirring overhead, Angelica, strapped into the worn seat, had desperate second thoughts about flying. An empty rectangle of air replaced the door on her father's side. She knew she should have more faith. He was a good pilot: no crashes ever in his army career flying Black Hawks, not even a near miss.

With a shuddering heave, the helicopter lifted from the ground and banked south, leaving the airfield, dusty road, and acres of coffee bushes and sugar cane far behind them. Tan beaches came into view, stretching between rocky inlets where giant turtles paddled in the turquoise sea. Stepping on the rudder pedal, her father swung the chopper's tail around, and they swooped back inland, circling into a northwesterly course. Plantations and rivers receded from sight as they flew over the Waimea Canyon and headed toward the rugged Na Pali coast.

"*Na Pali* means 'cliff,' " her father explained on the two-way intercom. "This region may have been the first part of Kauai ever to be settled. The islanders believe their ancestors still haunt these cliffs."

"Is that what you tell the tourists?"

"Yeah, they like to be spooked."

The cliffs plunged to a surf-streaked sea. A zodiac bumped through the spray, hugging the coastline of sandy coves and dark-mouthed grottos. Angelica pulled a camera from her bag and leaned toward her father's doorless side to take a picture while the chopper hovered in mid-air.

She would have liked to share the moment with Dex. Perhaps when she returned to Florida, they could pick up where they had left off. Meanwhile, she would savor every precious moment with her dad. Her family had all moved on with their lives—except her.

50

*T*he men in fuelling jumpsuits watched with studied nonchalance as the blonde bombshell strutted in spiked stilettos from the shiny limo to the shimmering Gulfstream jet poised for flight on the L.A. airfield.

Maynard Forbes followed his girlfriend, carrying an attaché case, but otherwise looking as though he were off to the Hamptons for the weekend, dressed as he was in crisp tennis whites, and sporting a tan. He ignored the attention Lindy attracted from the men on the tarmac as her micromini-molded hips swung up the steps to the plane. He was used to it.

Captain's hat pulled low over his face, Dex stood by the open door, the heady smell of diesel and baked macadam heightening the adrenalin rush as he waited to welcome the owner on board. He winked at Lindy and saluted Forbes. Lindy tensed, confusion blurring her pretty features. She turned to Maynard, too late. Already a man in a black suit, buzz-cut, and dark glasses had sprung from inside the jet. He manacled her bejeweled wrists while three of the ground crew, Glocks drawn, converged on Maynard at the foot of the steps.

"FBI!" yelled one of the men, flashing his badge.

51

*B*ehind designer sunglasses, the man scoped out Poipu Beach, where a seawater pool formed by a semi-circle of rocks provided a safe haven for squealing toddlers. The sand in front of Brenneckes Store & Restaurant accommodated a scattering of sunbathers, most of them couples. Angelica sat alone on a towel in a blue striped bikini and straw hat, reading a book and unaware she was being watched. But then, why should she suspect otherwise? She thought she had left that part of her life behind her.

*****

Angelica reached for the vibrating phone.

"Good news!" Kathy cried.

Angelica's heart missed a beat. "What happened?"

"You're never going to believe this, but the Epsteins signed the Plovers Key contract!"

Nothing had been further from Angelica's mind that morning, and it took a second for her to register what the office manager was talking about.

"It came in special delivery, marked for your attention."

"Any changes or contingencies?" Angelica asked cautiously.

"No, but Dr. Epstein scribbled something on a sticky note. His writing is so illegible it could be a prescription. But

228

I think I managed to decipher. Listen to this: 'As you can see, we still want the condo. Being a doctor and doctor's wife, we're not unduly fazed by the morbid circumstances. Best wishes, John and Isabel.' You did it, hon! I'll mail it on to Mrs. Bedford for her signature."

Angelica took a minute to absorb the news, which was as welcome as the Hawaiian sun warming her body. "Thanks for taking care of everything, Kathy. The next two lunches at Delilah's are on me. Did you tell Rick yet?"

"Don't worry, I'll break it to him gently," Kathy said with a chuckle.

"Anything else new at the office?"

"Well, Fred's all pimped because he wrote a contract for that commercial property on Industrial. Thursday is, after all, his most sober day. Nothing more for Rick so far. And a buyer made an offer on your Palm Meadow listing. Looks like Bill's office is yours, hon."

Angelica couldn't believe it and told Kathy so. The tide of luck had finally turned, bringing her ship to shore.

"How is Herx doing?" she asked.

"Fine, except that you really should get him seen to."

"Seen to?"

"Fixed. He humps my bunny slippers."

"Oh! Kathy, I'm so sorry."

"It's okay. It just makes it difficult to walk."

After promising to call the next day, Angelica put away her phone, smiling so hard at the vision of Hercules going at Kathy's slippers that the corners of her mouth began to ache. She was still grinning and trying to get back into *Demise in Paradise*, which she had bought for the trip, when a shadow fell across the pages.

She stared up at the stranger standing before her, his eyes masked by tinted sunglasses. Dressed in black shorts and T-shirt and carrying a black bag, he looked like a Mafia hit man disguised as a beach bum.

"Who are you?" she demanded when he made no effort to move.

"I was hoping for a better reception."

Recognizing the voice, Angelica scrambled to her feet. "Dex?" She pulled the sunglasses off his face. "You cut your hair!"

"Steady on!" he told her. "Those are Maui Jim shades and they cost a bomb at the airport."

"Well!" Angelica said, admiring him from every angle. "You look like Bon Jovi!" If she'd had to liken him to a rock star before, she would have had to say Meatloaf, but he had even lost a few pounds.

Dex beamed. "So you approve?" he asked, touching the back of his neck as though still trying to get used to the new style.

"What made you do it?"

He shrugged. "It was, like you said, a pain. So I donated my hair to an organization that makes wigs for cancer victims."

"Dex," she faltered, overcome with surprise at seeing him in Kauai, and so handsomely and charitably transformed.

"Enough about my hair," he murmured with becoming modesty. "Aren't you going to ask me what I'm doing here?"

"I was getting to that," she said, unable to take her eyes off him. "Would you like to sit down?"

"Thanks. I thought you'd never ask. I'm afraid I can't do much about the tattoo," he said, removing his T-shirt.

"I love your tattoo." She ran her fingertip over the silver Celtic cross.

"You do?"

"I do."

"Is there hope for us then, Angelica?" he declared in a mock-dramatic voice. "Because Marty said he could fly us up to a romantic spot in the mountains and—"

"You met my father?"

"Uh-huh. Cool guy. Totally laidback. Are you sure you're related?"

"Where did you see him?"

"In Hanapepe. Kathy told me your dad flew for Trans-Island Helicopters, and I found the address on their website. He said you'd be here."

"So why are *you* here? Truthfully."

"Truthfully, I was in L.A. The FBI nabbed Maynard and Lindy as they were about to take off for Southern Asia. I was posing as the pilot and saw everything. It was like a scene out of a movie. So now my mother is absolved of any wrongdoing."

"Your mother?"

"Bella."

"Bella Bedford?" Angelica cried. "Peter Bedford was your dad? Are you kidding me?"

"Calm down." Dex covered her hand with his. "He was my stepdad. I didn't like him much. I guess I felt resentful because I was still young when he married my mom. But he was good to me. He put me through college same as his own two kids."

His grip tightened on her hand. "Then I found out about his philandering. It was like a knife in my gut seeing what it was doing to Mom. So I helped her set him up. It wasn't very ethical, I admit, but it was the only way for her to get a divorce and maintain her expensive lifestyle. Peter was a tight-fisted bastard in some ways and made her sign a pre-nup."

"What about your real dad?"

"He was killed in a car accident when I was four."

"I'm sorry." Angelica scooped up a fistful of sand and watched it sift between her fingers, unable, suddenly, to look at him. "I didn't, you know, do more than kiss your stepfather . . ."

"I know."

"I'm so ashamed. I don't know what came over me."

"He could charm the birds off the trees."

She glanced at Dex, struck anew by how different he looked. "But that's why you followed me. To see if we were having an affair."

"At first. And then I followed you just because I wanted to. To make sure you were safe. I saw you briefly at the airport getting into a green car with a maniac."

"That was my sister. Anyway, you said I was boring!" She snatched her hand away.

"Hey. I said your life was boring. Not that *you* were. In fact, I've never had as much fun with anyone before."

Angelica stared at the towel, her heart beating faster. "So why did you keep running out on me?"

"Angelica, honey, I had a lot going on. I had to get my mom off the hook."

There was so much she wanted to say, but the honey part turned her brain to marshmallow. "Oh," she said, flopping onto her back and covering her eyes with her hands. *Reason for not calling, #14: He's busy protecting his mom from a murder charge.*

"What about that photo of Lindy?" she asked, holding on to the last bastion of defense against him.

"The one from the library? That wasn't Lindy! That was a photo of my mother in her beauty queen days, which she'd given to Peter. I didn't want the police getting hold of it and her getting in deeper. Are we straight now?"

Angelica nodded, smiling sheepishly.

"Good," Dex said, burrowing into his black tote bag. "One final thing. Detective Wright asked me to give you this." He handed her a small envelope.

Propping herself on an elbow, she tore it open and read the typewritten words:

"DEAR MS. LANE. MISPLACED MANILA ENVELOPE RECOVERED. MANY THANKS. CONTAINED RECORDS OF ILLEGAL WIRE TRANSFERS AND EVIDENCE OF CANINE SIDE EFFECTS IN LAB RATS AND HUMAN PATIENTS TESTED IN DEVELOPMENT OF EXPERIMENTAL PHEROMONE DRUG. SUSPECT APPREHENDED AND IN CUSTODY IN CONNECTION WITH BEDFORD'S MURDER.

PS. IN MY NON-PROFESSIONAL OPINION, YOUNG DEXTER CAN BE TRUSTED WITH ALL YOUR HEART. GOOD LUCK. BYRON WRIGHT."

Angelica stuck the note back in the envelope. "What was Forbes going to do in Asia?" she asked Dex.

"He has an offshore account in the Maldives where he salted away millions of rufiyaa. He and Lindy vacationed in Malé a couple of times. The islands don't have an extradition treaty with the U.S., far as I know."

"What will happen to Lindy?"

"She could end up in prison as well, for acting on Maynard's insider tip and selling her shares in his company."

Serves her right for trashing my car, Angelica thought.

"My stepdad discovered clinical trial data for Biche showing that eleven female humans developed a barking condition. But Maynard continued to tout it as a blockbuster product so he could continue to milk the company, and all the while he was unloading his shares. With the FDA about to make its decision public, the game was up, and he split."

Angelica savored the implications of what Dex had told her: The Bedford case was solved, and Forbes was in custody. She was in the clear.

"So you helped bring Maynard Forbes and Lindy to justice, and then followed me to Hawaii?"

"I know you said no more following, but, well, we never did have that dinner, and I'm a man of my word. But first," Dex said, grinning, "Want to guess what I have in this bag?"

A romantic lei of flowers? she wondered. Chilled champagne and glasses for two? Or perhaps a cuddly teddy bear with a bow he bought impulsively at the airport? Whatever it was, she was certain she would be thrilled.

"I can't begin to guess," she said.

Unzipping his black bag, Dex extracted two snorkels. "I have fins as well. You up for it?"

"Of course," Angelica said, although she would have been quite happy to stay with him on the towel. "Oh, hang on just a second." Retrieving her cell phone, she speed-dialed Kathy. "Can you get Rick if he's there?" she asked the office manager.

"Rick? Are you sure? I thought you wanted to be shot of this place for a while."

"Yeah, I'm sure. And thanks again, Kath."

A minute passed.

"Angelica!" Rick's voice resonated in her ear over the whoosh and rush of surf. "How you doing? Having fun?"

"Amazing. You?"

"Perfect."

Not for long, Angelica thought. "Listen, Rick, I wanted to let you know, in case you didn't yet, that I got the Plovers Key contract and an offer on my other listing." In the pause that followed, she imagined Rick choking as he realized he had lost the contest to her. "But I've decided to let you have Bill's office anyway," she told him.

Revenge was sweet, though ultimately not as satisfying as being gracious and magnanimous.

"I don't understand," Rick said sounding suspicious.

"I'll be spending less time at Plum Realty. I've decided to set up an office at home." She could afford to now. She might even go for her broker's license. "Bill's office is yours."

"That's very big of you, Angelica."

"I know. And just think how relieved Broker Bob will be. Anyway, I have to get off the phone. Pleasure calls."

"You have a date? What about us?"

"Bye, Rick."

She made a big production of turning off her phone and smiled at Dex. "I'm not even going to think about work anymore today," she said, gathering up her snorkeling gear.

They rinsed out their flippers at the water's edge and waded into the shallows, adjusting their masks. Dex dove into the transparent water and she followed, instantly transported into a world of colorful fish and coral flora. She felt as though she were floating around a giant aquarium as schools of butterfly fish fluttered by in choreographed elegance, and purple and yellow Tang, red Parrot, and balloon-size Bluefin Jack drifted past. Spotting a needlefish, she tugged on Dex's arm and pointed, and he took her hand in his.

52

*T*he next evening, after another day at the beach sunbathing and snorkeling, Dex and Angelica attended a luau with her father and his girlfriend. A luscious brunette with a sweet and shy disposition, the school teacher did her photo every justice, and she clearly adored Marty. Just as gratifying to Angelica, an instant bond had formed between him and Dex.

Seated at the trestle table amid a dozen others on the sand, the two of them shared beers and kalua pig roast—and the same wacky sense of humor. Male dancers in spinning grass skirts jabbed the air with spears on a stage lit by bamboo torches. More torches flamed in the surrounding darkness and flickered in the warm breeze imbued with smoke, the rush of surf accompanying the beat of Polynesian drums and convivial chatter.

The expectant mother sipped guava juice and protectively rubbed the slight mound of her stomach as she and Angelica discussed the forthcoming baby, to be named Martin Junior. Marty, alternating proud looks between his daughter and Nuala, beamed at everyone.

Their waist-long hair crowned with tropical flowers, women in swaying grass skirts and garlands replaced the prancing warriors and graced the stage with undulating arm gestures as they danced to the slow strum of ukuleles. Twiddling the straw in her Mai Tai, Angelica watched in distraction. Nothing could be more perfect than this moment, except that she had received some puzzling news from the office that day.

"What's up?" Dex asked from across the table. "You seem out of it, all of a sudden."

"I heard that the mother-in-law of one of my clients died while on a recent visit to Florida."

"Uh-oh."

The Peyntons had been renting a house while they hunted down their respective ideas of the ideal property. Now that the mother-in-law had been removed as the main obstacle to a mutually agreeable floor plan, Angelica supposed the task of finding Dick and Diane their dream home would be easier. Except that she had a niggling suspicion the death was no accident as Kathy had said on the phone.

"Uh-oh is right," she told Dex. "Broker Bob better not find out about it." She could see him sputtering right now. "He already called me on the carpet for your stepdad's murder and Rusty Scrob's arrest."

Scrob had skipped out on bail and never reclaimed his python, according to Detective Wright. The bank would in all probability repossess the eyesore on Flamingo Circle, leaving Jenn out of a commission, and Broker Bob even more furious.

Dex took her hand in his. "Hey. There's nothing you can do about it for now. And none of it is your fault anyway. So you might as well let it go."

She looked at Nuala and Marty, feeding each other forkfuls of lomi salmon and sweet potato from the banquet. "You're absolutely right," she replied with a wide smile. "I'm supposed to be on vacation."

And perhaps Dick Peynton's large mother-in-law *had* accidentally drowned in the hot tub.

Epilogue

A rainbow trapped in the mountain valley cast diffuse colors on the waterfall cascading down the ravine. As they stepped out of the helicopter, Reverend Matsuaki told Angelica the rainbow was an excellent omen and that water flowing out of the rock was considered holy on the island.

Dex descended next in black pants and a white embroidered shirt, blond hair brushed back from his tanned face. Angelica had never seen him look more handsome.

She gazed around the small gathering, at her father, arms around his girlfriend, slimmer now after the birth of their child; bridesmaids Claire and Sam in long white tunics accessorized with arm bracelets; her mom, wearing a wide hat, and stepdad, Dave, both still green from the chopper ride up the mountain; and Bella dressed in a Chanel suit, smiling serenely in the company of Dex's younger half-sister and half-brother, who so resembled Peter Bedford with his reddish-blond hair and boyish grin that Angelica found the sight of him quite unnerving.

She only regretted that her friends from Plum Realty could not be here with her. On the phone the day before, Kathy described the office party she had arranged in honor of Angelica's nuptials. The event had been a blast, and although Broker Bob stipulated that no alcohol be consumed on the premises, Fred spiked the punch with vodka, and everyone got tipsy, especially Fred, while Bill Bungle fell asleep over the photo copy machine. Rick and Gloria disappeared for twenty minutes into Rick's new office where someone jokingly taped the motivational message, "Just do it!" on the door. Jenn and young Tyler left together, and Kathy confided that Phil had gone home with her, which didn't go over well with Hercules, who barked so distractingly outside the bedroom door that she had to put him in the yard, where he proceeded to dig up the perennials.

However, he was quite good at the party, Kathy had assured Angelica. Broker Bob, who couldn't be more pleased with all the new clients that Angelica had brought to Plum Realty from Bella's wide sphere of Manalo-heeled friends, solved the problem of Hercules lunging for Rick by muzzling the dog with his red silk bowtie, the moment captured for posterity in the framed photo that Kathy was giving as her wedding present.

The guests snapped pictures on the mountainside while the minister took his place before the bride and groom to-be. Angelica felt the light spray from the waterfall in her hair that Claire had curled that morning. Her frothy white dress rippled in the breeze, her veil, secured by a diamond tiara, billowing around her. On escorting Angelica to the helicopter pad, her father had declared her to be "a perfect princess" and, for the first time in her life, that was precisely how she felt.

The minister cleared his throat with a formal cough and spoke a few words of greeting in Hawaiian. Dex smiled down at his future wife, his slate gray eyes twinkling in the sunlight as, dizzy with love, Angelica tried not to lose her balance on the pebbly slope.

"Today," Reverend Matsuaki began, "is a special day in your lives as you come to this beautiful island of Kauai to be united in marriage before God and these witnesses. I pray God's blessings of health, strength and prosperity be yours all the days of your lives. And with that," he announced with a broad smile, "let the celebration begin!"

READ ON FOR AN EXCERPT OF

Murder at the Dolphin Inn

A Rex Graves Mystery

The Dolphin Inn

Key West, FL

#1, McCullers Suite ~ Bill Reid

#2, Tennessee Williams Suite ~ Mae & Emily Hart

#3, Hemingway Suite ~ Diane S. Dyer

#4, Jimmy Buffet Suite ~ Dennis & Peggy Barber

#5, Robert Frost Suite ~ vacant

#6, Audubon Suite ~ Chuck & Alma Shumaker

#7, Writer's Garret ~ Michelle Cuzzens & Ryan Ford

#8, Poet's Attic ~ vacant

~ONE~

*G*ift-wrapped in yellow ribbon, the Dolphin Inn stood amid a lush landscape abloom with orchids, red-spiked bromeliads, and Chinese Palm fans. White porches decorated with gingerbread trim wrapped long arms around the lilac clapboard, while a transom window depicting frolicking blue dolphins topped the Victorian mansion's front door. Hard to imagine a double homicide taking place here, Rex thought. The bed-and-breakfast was, to use a British expression, rather "twee."

Geckos skittered before his sandals on the brick path that led to a white picket fence separating the property from the street, where he had left his fiancée among a crowd of onlookers. Undeterred by the traffic cones, their number had increased in the half hour or so since he had been inside the guest house. There would doubtless have been more spectators had it not been the morning after the annual Fantasy Fest Parade, a night of heavy drinking and revelry, which he and Helen had missed as they sailed from Miami to Mallory Square on a Carnival cruise ship.

Empty beer cans and strings of iridescent beads littered the sun-dappled sidewalks of the street. Rex derived no small measure of satisfaction thinking that the fall weather back home in Scotland would be gray and drizzly; not balmy as here in Key West. Dressed for the most part in slogan T-shirts, shorts, and sunglasses, the rubberneckers formed an almost comical contrast to the dark-uniformed and serious-countenanced city cops on duty displaying the blue and gold patches of the KWPD on their sleeves.

"He really fancies himself, doesn't he?" Helen said, nodding in the direction of the patrol officer on guard outside the gate. His upper body was muscle-bound to the point of diminished mobility, and he wore a wide brimmed hat cocked jauntily on his head, his black holster polished to the patina of glass. "Is it true the two dead bodies are dressed up as clowns?" she asked.

"Aye," Rex replied in his Lowland Scots. He had just seen them. Hands bound, plastic bags over their heads, they sat slumped on the floor of the kitchen. "Merle and Taffy Dyer, owners of the bed-and-breakfast. Died of asphyxiation, it would appear."

"Who did you speak to?"

"Captain Dan Diaz, the ranking detective. Pleasant chap, but not verra forthcoming. As to be expected." Rex conceded the man had a lot on his hands.

"I was talking to someone called Mike, an innkeeper on Francis Street. Handsome devil. He was quite chatty," Helen added with a pleased smile.

"You mean he tried to chat you up."

"He told me the owners had been running the Dolphin Inn for six years, after selling their bed-and-breakfast in Vermont. She was an alcoholic, and her husband a controlling miser. Seems the son hated his parents with a vengeance. The daughter is recently divorced and brought her two whiny children to stay while she got back on her feet."

"This Mike knows a lot."

"He said the Key West Association of Innkeepers is a very tight-knit community."

"So it would seem."

Reporters gathered even as they watched. The double murder of two respectable citizens was big news. A pod of marked and unmarked vehicles nosing the curb offloaded EMS personnel, while two-way radios emitted a steady stream of flat-toned static. A wave of tension rippled through the crowd.

"Seems a bit ghoulish standing here waiting for the body bags to be carried out to the morgue," Helen remarked. "There's loads to see in Key West, and we only have a few hours before we have to get back on our ship."

"Och, we're not really going to get back on that floating monstrosity, are we?"

"What do you mean?" his fiancée asked, stiffening in her yellow sun dress.

"I mean, the cabin is stifling and I bumped my head getting out of bed this morning. Plus, our waiter looks and sounds like a poor imitation of Dracula. Where do they find these people?"

"He's Romanian."

"Transylvania used to be in Romania, didn't it?"

Helen tried to suppress a smile, and failed miserably. "So, what do you suggest, exactly?"

"Let's retrieve our luggage and stay in Key West."

"But what about Mexico?"

"What aboot it?"

"I wanted to sample some real margaritas."

"We can get margaritas here. Jimmy Buffet made Key West the Margaritaville of the world."

"But it's a free cruise," Helen insisted. She had won it in a sweepstakes on a previous cruise to the Caribbean.

"All the more reason to chuck it," Rex pointed out. He had only agreed to the cruise with great reluctance. "And the return voyage doesn't bear thinking aboot—two full days at sea watching hairy chest contests on deck." He couldn't imagine anything worse.

Helen's face dissolved into a mischievous grin. "I was going to enter you! Ah, well." She sighed in capitulation. "So what do we do now? Assuming we can get out of the cruise…"

"Find a place to stay."

Helen consulted her tourist map. "Mike's bed-and-breakfast is on Frances Street. He told me he's always fully booked in October, but he may be able to recommend somewhere."

"What aboot here?"

"What do you mean, Rex?" The tone in which she said "Rex" did not bode well for his plans.

"There's a vacancy. The innkeeper said he'd offer us a discount."

"I should think so," she exploded. "It's a murder scene!"

"Could have been a suicide pact," he said to placate her.

"You don't think that for a moment. I know you. You want to stay here so you can solve the murders. I cannot believe this!" She put her foot down, literally, stomping her sandaled foot on the pavement.

Rex gazed with regret at the lilac façade of the guest house. "You're right, lass. This was supposed to be a romantic trip. But the bodies are in a separate part of the house, and there's no blood or mess whatsoever." Just two shrink-wrapped heads. "It's squeaky clean," he assured her.

Helen shot him a sardonic look. "Surprising the police would let the guests stay," she remarked.

"Why not? Easier to keep an eye on everybody that way. And, as I said, the bodies are in an annex, closed off from the rest of the premises by a passageway."

"How can you be so nonchalant?"

"Just practical. And you'll like this: The suites are named after famous writers who lived or stayed in Key West. Hemingway, Tennessee Williams…" Rex, having forgotten the others, brandished the B & B brochure in his hand and looked at her hopefully.

The wind appeared to go out of her sails as she exhaled a deep breath. "What would we have to do to cancel our cruise?"

"The innkeeper's son said he would contact the cruise line. We simply retrieve our bags and let the *Fantasia* set sail without us. I'll go back in and see what he managed to arrange," Rex said before she could change her mind.

If they stayed, he might even get the chance to see his son again before they returned to the UK. Pursuing his studies in marine science in Jacksonville, Campbell had met up with his dad and Helen in Miami for an all too brief visit.

"I heard there's great shopping on Duval Street…" Helen held out her palm.

Grinning, Rex extracted his American Express card from his wallet, and she flicked it out of his fingers.

"Thank you!" she chirped. "Meet you back here at eleven."

Encircling her waist, he kissed her on the ear. "You're a great sport, Helen."

"So you keep telling me. I just hope I don't live to regret this."

Christmas Is Murder

Starred Review from *Booklist:*

The first installment in this new mystery series is a winner. The amateur detective is Rex Graves, a Scottish barrister, fond of Sudoku puzzles and Latin quotations. In an old-fashioned conceit, Challinor begins with a cast of characters, along with hints of possible motives for each. Although set firmly in the present, this tale reads like a classic country-house mystery. Rex and the others are snowed in at the Swanmere Manor hotel in East Sussex, England. Being the last to arrive, Rex immediately hears of the unexpected demise of one of the other guests. By the time the police arrive days later, additional bodies have piled up and motives are rampant, but Rex has identified the murderer. At times, it seems we are playing Clue or perhaps enjoying a contemporary retelling of a classic Agatha Christie tale *(And Then There Were None,* or *At Bertram's Hotel)* with a charming new sleuth. A must for cozy fans.

Murder in the Raw

Mystery Scene Magazine:

In *Murder in the Raw*, Scottish barrister Rex Graves must expose—and I do mean expose—the killer of Sabine Durand, a French actress who goes missing one evening from a nudist resort in the Caribbean... Set on an island, *Murder in the Raw* is a clever variant on the locked room mystery, and Rex discovers that everyone in this self-contained locale has a secret when it comes to the intriguing Sabine. Who, though, would benefit from her disappearance or murder? With a host of colorful characters, a dose of humor and a balmy locale, you will want to devour this well-plotted mystery. I won't spoil your pleasure by divulging the solution, but suffice it to say that Challinor provides a most compelling answer.

Phi Beta Murder*

Foreword Magazine:

Readers meet up once again with Rex Graves in the third mystery to follow the Scottish barrister with a knack for getting involved in the ultimate crime. Rex is on his way out of the beautiful Scottish countryside leaving behind Helen, his new woman friend and his mother to visit his son on the campus of his American college. Campbell Graves is supposed to be enjoying life at Hilliard University in Jacksonville, Florida, but lately on the phone he's sounded rather distant, and Rex wants nothing more than to see his son and make sure everything is all right. Unfortunately the day he steps on campus is the day a young man is found in his locked room hanging from the ceiling. Soon Rex must split his time between worrying about his son, solving a crime that seems to involve a million people with a million different agendas, and trying to balance his love life without losing people in the process. Humor and well-written characters add to the story, as does some reflection on the causes of suicide. A wonderful read and great plot for cozy mystery lovers.

* This title has not been endorsed by the Phi Beta Kappa Society. The Phi Beta Kappa fraternity depicted in the novel is in no way affiliated nor associated with the Phi Beta Kappa Society.

Murder on the Moor

BellaOnline:

Scottish Barrister and amateur sleuth Rex Graves purchased Gleneagle Lodge so that he and his girlfriend, Helen D'Arcy, could get away to spend some private time together. Now he wonders why he had agreed to host a housewarming party for several acquaintances and friends. When one of the guests turns up dead, her body found in a nearby loch, the finger-pointing begins. Graves cannot help but put his sleuthing skills to work as he tries to find out who killed his house guest while he also gathers clues as to who is committing the so-called Moor Murders. He is wondering if the two are tied and if he is hosting the killer. When a storm prevents anyone from leaving, Rex and Helen do their best to keep everyone calm during their forced confinement. Set in the Scottish Highlands, Challinor successfully utilizes the atmosphere of the countryside to enhance the tension going on inside the Lodge. The characters seem typical of the type seen in many mysteries written by such authors as Agatha Christie, and are a welcome diversion from today's style of writing. The writing is crisp and the story fast-paced. The inevitable gathering of the guests in the library comes with a twist or two, and the ending is a satisfying conclusion to a solid who-dun-it.

Murder of the Bride

Buried Under Books:

Rex Graves is back, this time visiting his fiancée, Helen
d'Arcy, so they can attend the wedding in Aston-on-Trent of
one of her former students. Polly Newcombe is very pregnant
and her groom, Timmy Thorpe looks a bit peaked, but is it just
the dreary day leading Rex to think the success of this
marriage is doubtful? Perhaps not, as the reception at the
bride's family country home in Derbyshire soon turns from a
pleasant celebration to a scene of mayhem when Polly
collapses, looking more than a little green. Leaving the
reception and heading to Aston-on-Trent, Rex learns a great
deal more about the secrets of the Newcombe and Thorpe
families. Is jealousy behind the attacks? Greed? Infidelity?
Overbearing mothers? Rex and the local police have an
overabundance of clues and evidence, and getting to the
solution to the case will require much thought and
cooperation. This latest case for Rex Graves is every bit as
charming and entertaining as those in earlier books and
readers will not be disappointed. The setting, an English
country home, is as much a character as the people, and
many of those characters are a delight, especially Police
Constable Perrin (and the cast of characters provided by the
author is very much appreciated).

ABOUT THE AUTHOR

C.S. Challinor was born in Bloomington, Indiana, and was educated in Scotland and England. She now lives in Southwest Florida where she has sold real estate for seven years. She is the author of the Rex Graves cozy mystery series featuring Rex Graves, a Scottish barrister-sleuth.

All Rex Graves titles (one through five published by Midnight Ink Books) are available in trade paperback, Kindle, Nook, etc. *Christmas Is Murder*, the first in the series, is also available in LP hardcover (Thorndike Reviewer's Choice). *Murder of the Bride* was selected as a Mystery Guild Book Club pick (hardcover).

Visit the author at ***www.rexgraves.com***.